# TARGET ACQUIRED

## ED GRACE

**Blood Splatter Press**

# ALSO BY ED GRACE

## Titles in the Jay Sullivan Series

Assassin Down

Kill Them Quickly

The Bars That Hold Me

A Deadly Weapon

Target Acquired

The End of a Life (Novella)

# NEW JERSEY, US

# CHAPTER ONE

THE MAN CROSSED AND UNCROSSED HIS LEGS AS HE fidgeted with his tie.

Walter couldn't help but smile.

He loved how his appearance made people uncomfortable. Whether it was the skinhead, the white vest, or the Arian Alliance patch clinging to his tatty jeans by two pins, he enjoyed watching disapproving middle-class men in suits squirm.

"Well, erm, well, you see, I, er..." the man said, clicking the mouse a few times whilst staring at the computer screen. "It's just not, erm, it's—it's, er, bad news, I'm afraid."

Walter glanced at the nameplate on the guy's desk. His name was Eugene. Walter once had an uncle called Eugene. He'd hated the man.

"Why don't you just spit it out?" Walter then leant forward, looked deep into Eugene's wide, blue eyes that appeared magnified beneath large spectacles, and spoke with a quiet husk, "Tell me whether I can, or I can't."

Eugene gulped. Ran a hand over his neatly parted hair. He took a moment, then blurted out, "I'm afraid I can't permit you international travel," and stared at Walter, waiting for the reaction he feared.

"Would you mind repeating that?" Walter said, sitting back in his chair with his legs open, taking up as much space as possible. "I didn't quite hear you."

"Well, you see, I am afraid I can't permit you international travel. Not with a record like this."

"What exactly is it about my record that is so bad?"

"Well, I can see multiple counts of assault, threats on government officials, inciting violence during the Charlottesville rally—"

"Is that proven?"

"Excuse me?"

"The Unite the Right rally. I didn't run down no one with my car, did I?"

"No, but you were charged with disturbing the peace. And, to add to that, you're still on license since being released from prison for hate crime."

Walter grinned. It was like someone reading out a menu of his favourite food. He was practically salivating.

"I mean, shall I go on?"

"Please."

Eugene shook his head. Apparently, the question was rhetorical. "I'm not sure what you were expecting, Mr Franks, but we can't grant you international—"

Walter slammed his fist on the table. Pencil pots and papers shook, and Eugene jumped.

"I think you just have a problem with me, personally, don't you?"

Eugene's lip quivered. His body stiffened. He obviously wished to say yes; that Walter was a racist, and that of course he hated him. As far as Walter was concerned, Eugene was like the other cowards who weren't prepared to stand up for their heritage; who'd support the wishes of inferior races to be equal to those with an inherent right to this country. Walter could even imagine Eugene watching immigrants move into a pleasant family home across the street—one that could have gone to a decent American family—and saying nothing. He wouldn't show the rage Walter harnessed; he'd suppress it under the false pretence of 'an equal society.'

It was bullshit.

But this wasn't the time for debate. Walter was fed up with talking. People like Eugene never listened. It was time for action; time to educate people about the truth. Hence the reason Walter wished to travel to the UK to demonstrate his beliefs; a country that had been America's ally for so long, but had become far too tolerant of minorities. There comes a time when it is crucial to cut such traitors loose, and Walter wished to travel to the UK to make his opinion clear.

But first, he needed the passport, and Eugene was not being cooperative.

"I assure you, this is not personal," Eugene lied.

"And is there nothing you can do about this?" Walter asked.

"I'm afraid not."

"You'll regret it."

Walter sat still for a moment. His fingers interlocked. Staring at Eugene with a calm that only increased the man's fear.

Eugene did not meet Walter's eyes.

"I need this passport, Eugene."

"I understand that, but—"

"I don't think you do. Perhaps I should make you understand."

Walter glanced at a photograph of Eugene's family on the edge of the desk. His wife was overweight and frowning. His child looked dorky. Walter imagined that, if he was still a child, he would have probably ended up bullying Eugene's son. It is a crucial characteristic of a predator to prey on the weak; it keeps the natural order of the food chain intact.

"Can I show you out?" Eugene eventually said.

Walter knew this exchange wasn't going anywhere, but he still didn't move. He was enjoying intimidating this man. The feeling of power it gave him was almost addictive.

Eventually, Walter said, "That would be great."

Eugene stood and led him to the door. Walter walked out and turned to Curtis, who sat on a plastic chair in the waiting room.

Ah, Curtis. More devoted to the cause than anyone. A true comrade, loyal to the end, waiting for Walter with his hand resting on his balls and a cigarette perched between his lips.

"Excuse me," Eugene said, "but you're not allowed to smoke in here."

Walter chuckled. Eugene didn't know who he was messing with, and Walter enjoyed seeing the look on Eugene's face as he took in Curtis's appearance.

Curtis's pupils were tattooed completely black, whilst the tattoos on his skin started from the top of his shaved head and ended beneath his boots. Walter watched Eugene recognise the symbols marked on Curtis's body—from the 88 beside his eye, to the eagle atop his skull, to the crossed grenades on his neck, to the swastika over his shoulder—and sniggered as Eugene tried to hide his disapproval.

Curtis stood, squared up to Eugene, and barely a sound made it past the posh man's lips. Eugene was evidently trying to stay strong, but his knees were buckling.

Eugene went to speak again, but Curtis halted him by stretching his neck forward and making a bizarre bird noise an inch from Eugene's face. As Eugene stared back, Curtis tapped him on the shoulder, as if reassuring a child that it was okay that he'd lost on sport's day, and moseyed into Eugene's office.

"Excuse me, but that is my–"

Curtis raised his hand, and Eugene fell silent. Curtis inhaled his cigarette, then held it between his fingers as he surveyed the desk and chairs and filing cabinets. He placed the cigarette back between his lips, took hold of the edge of the desk, lifted it, and threw it upside down, forcing the computer screen to smash against the radiator. Eugene could only watch in horror as Curtis then lifted a chair and hurled it at the far wall, leaving a dent in the plaster, before unzipping his flies and pissing over Eugene's comfortable leather seat.

Once he finished, Curtis strolled out of the office with a cocky strut, paused by Eugene, spat his cigarette at the man's face, then ran the backs of his urine-stained hands down Eugene's suit, before turning his hands over and drying his palms.

He gave Eugene a nod goodbye and left.

Walter sighed and said, "I said you'd regret it," and followed Curtis out.

# CHAPTER TWO

Hours later, Walter was still seething. As he sat in his favourite pub, a beer on the bar in front of him, and Curtis playing with his lighter and a beer mat beside him, Walter rested his head on his fist and stared at the bottles of spirits organised neatly against the wall.

How can he show these people how wrong they are?

When Trump had made it into power, he'd felt a surge of hope. The man spoke sense. He despised immigrants. His response to Charlottesville was fair; he'd emphasised that there were bad people on both sides. And, what's more, he was planning to do things about it, like building a wall or halting immigration from several Islamic countries.

And now he was gone. No wall had been built, and no one even acknowledged that the election was rigged. And Joe Biden, the sycophantic bastard who'd robbed the position as president, had stood there, at his inauguration, claiming it was time to heal.

To heal from what?

They had it right a few hundred years ago.

Their brains are smaller. Fact.

They commit more crime. Fact.

They don't belong here. Fact.

Every time the superior race looked like they were close to taking their country back, some self-righteous liberal hippies counter protested. They claimed black lives matter, like white lives don't. They claimed we should let all the immigrants in, as if they don't taint this country. And yet they marginalised people like him for standing against them and speaking the truth.

That was why his mission was so important.

The UK was the same; they'd shown hope. They left Europe and told the immigrants to fuck off. Walter was delighted. And then what happened? They let in Iranians, Iraqis, Albanians, and the Sudanese. As if them sailing across the sea in a tiny boat means their desperation makes them worthy. As if the fucked-up state of their country didn't show what they were capable of.

The US was being taught its lesson. Now it was time to take their lessons overseas.

But first he had to get there.

A set of black fingers drummed against the bar next to him. A man paused beside him, waiting to be served. Walter's eyes rose to this man's dark skin and bright white teeth, and he felt a pang of disgust glowering inside of him.

"Hi there," the man said, smiling at Walter.

Walter felt rage soaring through him, buzzing down his arms, shaking his legs. His hand tightened around his beer glass, and he considered how much effort it would take to smash the glass and use the shard to slit this guy's throat.

Sixty years ago, a black man wouldn't dare be in the same bar as him, never mind speak to him. What the fuck has happened since?

The man shifted under Walter's gaze, offering an awkward smile. Walter knew he was staring. He didn't care.

"Where you from, boy?" Walter asked.

The man flinched when Walter said *boy*. This gave Walter a tinge of delight.

"Excuse me?"

"I said, where are you from?"

"Detroit."

"No, I mean before then."

The man looked confused. "I don't know what you mean."

"I mean, where did you come from before Detroit?"

"Nowhere. That's where I was born."

Walter snorted. The barman served the man as Walter chuckled sarcastically.

"Your mother took up our hospital space to give birth to you too, I guess," he muttered. "Came over to bring another one of you into the world... Fucking ingrates."

The barman placed a drink in front of the man.

"And where's your mama from?" Walter persisted.

"Listen, I just want my drink, I don't want any—"

"I don't give a shit what you want. You're in our country, in our bars, drinking our beers, so you will answer our fucking questions. Where was your mama from?"

"Detroit."

"Before that?"

"She lived in Detroit."

"But she weren't born there, was she? Where was it? Ghana? Tibet? Some fucking African country?"

The man lifted his drink, turned, paused, and seemed to consider replying. Instead, he just added, "You have a good day," and turned away.

Walter was off his bar stool before he could even fathom what his drunken mind had planned.

"Don't you turn away from me, boy!"

The man turned back. "What is your problem?" he asked.

Then the man saw Curtis. The eyes. The tattoos. The

hunched back, the bony physique, the look of insanity twisted with menace in the way he held his body. His lip twitched and his neck twisted to the side.

"Listen, I don't want any trouble," the man said.

Curtis raised his eyebrows, stretching the 88 beside his eye and the grenade tattooed beside the other.

"You're obviously into some racist shit," the man continued, "and good for you, if that's what you want to believe, but guys, seriously, I'm not interested. I'm really not. I just want to have my drink in peace and—"

In a burst of anger, Curtis turned the nearest table upside down, forcing several glasses to smash and a young couple to leap up from their seats.

The entire pub fell silent. Everyone looked from one face to the other. Some probably considered intervening, but then they saw Curtis's appearance, and opted to protect themselves rather than help the man.

Walter loved how much Curtis's appearance scared people. He knew Curtis at school, and no one would have feared the scraggly little misfit then—now, the fear he inspired was almost legendary.

"What do you want?" the man continued. "If it's a fight, then I don't want it. Really, I don't."

Curtis's head twisted to the side. His tongue flickered out. He'd had it surgically split in two. It looked beautifully vile.

"Look, man," the man said. "I can see you're obviously into all this—"

Curtis leapt forward, like a tiger on its prey, and placed his spindly fingers around the man's throat as he took him to the ground.

Curtis lifted his other hand, raising his long, infected fingernails high above him, and went to strike the black man's jaw.

But he couldn't.

Someone had a hand around his wrist.

Curtis looked up, amazed that someone would dare. He rose from the floor, staring at the stranger gripping his arm.

The stranger didn't falter from his position. He stood tall. He looked drunk, his eyebrows were drooping a bit, but he still seemed confident. He'd probably been in a few fights before.

But it was unlikely he'd ever been in a fight with a man like Curtis.

"You don't want to do that," Curtis sang out.

"Yeah," replied Jay Sullivan. "I think I do."

# CHAPTER THREE

SULLIVAN ALWAYS SEEMED TO END UP IN THE SAME PUB AS these idiots.

He wasn't sure whether he attracted them, whether they were just everywhere, or whether it was simply the kind of establishments he found himself in—he chose seedy bars so that anyone who might recognise him wouldn't rat him out—but he was growing tired of coming across them.

The man in question had an appearance unlike Sullivan had ever seen before, and Sullivan had seen it all throughout the years: Somalian pirates; tattooed tribes in the jungle; fetish whores catering for corrupt politicians; gangs in Kenya, Belize, East Timor, Honduras, Guatemala—but he had never seen a man who looked as messed up as this.

During his time as a brainwashed, trained assassin, murdering people across the globe for what he believed was his patriotic duty, he had come across neo-Nazis who dressed like this man; who thought they were standing up for their race, and didn't realise they were doing nothing else but adding even more tension to an already precarious situation.

But he had never met a Nazi who'd gone so far as to tattoo their pupils black.

Normally, a swastika or an SS symbol tattoo might be visible on their chest or bicep, but this man had decorated himself head-to-toe in symbols of blatant and little-known racist origin. Whilst many people would recognise the swastika, only people with knowledge of the most deprived corners of the world would recognise the KKK's blood drop on his cheek, or the Othala Rune on his hand, or the secret dice on his neck. The dice, in particular, might look to most like a pair of dice—but, as Sullivan glared at the man's throat, he saw a hidden message for other racists; on the left dice, a tile with a single dot, and a tile with four dots, meaning 1 and 4. On the other dice were five dots and three dots, meaning 88. 14 represents the slogan of white supremacy; that they must secure the future of the white children; and the 88 represents the phrase *Heil Hitler*.

Sullivan despised everything about this man, and he had to do all he could to resist pounding this prick's head into the bar until he was dead. Sullivan assumed the guy had little experience of the world beyond his own sheltered upbringing, yet still believed he had some kind of profound statement to make. He was probably once a lost child, a loner at school, much like Sullivan, and would have found comfort in the wrong people, also much like Sullivan. The difference was that Sullivan had realised his mind had been warped.

"Let go of my fucking hand," the bloke said. His voice sounded like the kind of voice mad people hear whispering to them at night.

Sullivan didn't let go, if only to prove that he had the power. He was also quite drunk, but hadn't realised it until now. The room was spinning, and this man was out of focus. He was used to fighting, however, and being highly inebriated had never stopped him from kicking someone's arse before.

"Hey, I know you," his opponent said, narrowing his eyes. "Holy shit, yes—you're Jay Sullivan! I thought you were dead, man."

"Curtis," said the other guy. Also dressed like a skinhead, though he didn't appear as vile as the one he referred to as Curtis. "I don't give a shit who he is. He thinks he's standing up for the negro."

"The what?" Sullivan gripped Curtis's wrist harder. "What did you just call him?"

"My friend," the black man said, putting a hand on Sullivan's shoulder. "It is not worth it."

But Sullivan was already too involved.

"I think you ought to take that back," Sullivan stated.

Curtis's mouth curled upwards, and he laughed. He sounded like a dying parrot.

This guy did not know who he was fucking with.

"Trust me," Sullivan said. "I am—"

Before Sullivan could boast about his credentials, Curtis had leapt upwards, faster than Sullivan's intoxicated mind could register, and clamped his teeth around Sullivan's wrist. Sullivan's fingers instinctively loosened their grip, but Curtis did not. Sullivan shook his arm like it was on fire, but Curtis held on, and held on, and held on, until Sullivan's blood was dribbling down the psycho's chin.

Sullivan, trying to quell his temper, swung his other fist into Curtis's head, knocked him off his wrist, then grabbed Curtis by the back of the neck and slammed his face into the bar.

Curtis laughed. Sullivan slammed the dickhead's face into the bar again, and the guy kept laughing, his manic cackles filling the pub.

This wasn't the reaction people normally had to taking a beating.

Sullivan went to lift Curtis's head again, but Curtis turned his body and threw his fist at Sullivan. Sullivan went to block the strike to his chest as if he was fighting a trained professional, but Curtis's fighting prowess came from the dirty tactics he used on the streets, not martial arts, and Sullivan did not predict that Curtis would open his fist, take hold of Sullivan's scrotum, and squeeze it harder and harder until Sullivan was terrified the fucker was going to pull his balls clean off.

Sullivan swiped a hand into Curtis's elbow, forcing it to bend, and hopefully release his grip—but Curtis simply knelt to avoid releasing the balls. Sullivan twisted his arm around Curtis's arm, straightened his muscles, and pushed his opponent's body away, finally forcing Curtis to release his hold.

Curtis lay on the floor, holding his belly to contain the force of his laughter.

"You little shit!" Sullivan barked, stumbling slightly—he was still wasted—and grabbed Curtis's shirt, lifted him, then lunged him headfirst into the bar.

Curtis, however, did not make an impact on the bar. He turned his body so his back collided with the bar instead, and landed on his knees. He placed one foot against the bar and used it to push himself forward, into Sullivan, taking them both to the floor too quick for Sullivan's drunken mind to make sense of it. He landed atop Sullivan with his hands around his neck.

Before Sullivan's drunken delay could make sense of his next move, Curtis's teeth were on his neck, and they were digging deep, searching for a windpipe.

Sullivan, feeling the warmth of his blood trickling down his Adam's apple, pushed himself to his knees. He lifted Curtis off the ground and, with him still attached to his neck, ran into the nearest wall so Curtis's head would make impact.

Curtis's canines loosened grip, and Sullivan threw the bastard off.

He stood, pressing against the wound on his neck, feeling the blood trickle between his fingers.

The world grew fuzzy. He stumbled into a table and tried to keep balance. Something smashed against the back of his head. A bottle, maybe. Sullivan wasn't sure. He fell to his knees, trying desperately to stay conscious, but failing.

The next thing he knew, he was regaining focus again, and he was on his back, and there was laughter, lots of demented laughter.

He tried getting to his feet, but he fell back, and someone kicked him, and he went stumbling out of the pub door, into the night, falling onto his front, losing consciousness as his face landed in something smelly.

When he came around later, he realised it was dog shit.

# CHAPTER FOUR

"HERE, LET ME HELP YOU."

Sullivan's eyes opened. The moon was bright. Or did it just seem bright?

"Over here, come on."

A muscular arm tucked around Sullivan's waist. He tried to push it away, but his arms wouldn't respond. He found himself walking, the ground spinning beneath his feet, until the stranger placed him on a bench.

He went to look up at his helper, but a mouthful of sick lurched to his throat and his entire body convulsed before he was able. A lumpy bile soared through his mouth and landed on his shoes; a pair of Berlutis that used to be pristine.

"Jesus. Come on, I'm going to get you to a hospital."

"No!"

Sullivan pushed the man away. He looked up to see who it was. It was the guy he defended in the pub, although Sullivan wasn't sure whether that had happened a few minutes ago, or a few hours ago.

"You're going to choke on your vomit if I leave you here."

"I'll be fine."

"No, you won't."

Sullivan chuckled. "Trust me, mate—I've gotten fucked and thrown up plenty of times."

"That may be true, but—"

"Honestly, I don't care if I choke on it. Just leave me alone."

"I really can't—"

"Just fuck off!"

Sullivan glared at the man. He knew he should appreciate the guy's help, but he'd just taken an arse kicking for him—he owed the guy no further politeness.

The man stood over him, staring.

Sullivan blinked away a head rush, and noticed that the man had quite a perplexed expression on his face.

"Where do I know you from?" the man asked.

"Nowhere."

Sullivan turned away. Used the bench to help himself up. Stumbled down the street.

"Can I at least get you home?" the man asked.

Sullivan snorted. "There is no home."

He used a nearby tree to steady himself, then stumbled to the right, and to the left, then fell, his hands landing in mud.

The man reached out to help balance Sullivan, and as he did, Sullivan noticed an FBI badge inside the man's jacket. He couldn't help scoffing. If he'd have known this guy was a fed, he wouldn't have bothered helping him. He despised the FBI —not just because they were hunting him, but because they were all meatheads who weren't worth saving. They cared more about their careers than the people they swore to save. He'd hesitate to piss on one if they were on fire.

The man placed his hand on Sullivan's back, and he knocked it away.

"Do you not take a hint?"

The man still stared at Sullivan with that look on his face.

"Really, I think I know you."

Sullivan didn't like being recognised.

It didn't feel good.

For all Sullivan knew, he could have murdered the guy's family, or he could have been part of a team tracking Sullivan. Either way, Sullivan wanted to get away from this man before he realised why he recognised Sullivan.

"I've done this a lot," Sullivan said, desperate to get away. "This is just a Tuesday evening for me."

"I know, but I–"

"Really, I'll be fine."

"But–"

"I'm fine!"

Sullivan pushed the man's arm away for the final time and continued down the street, crossing an empty road, then using a closed liquor store to steady himself before floundering further down the pavement.

Then he remembered he was in America, and wondered if he should call it a sidewalk, then laughed at a thought that wasn't actually that funny.

He didn't recall what happened next.

Perhaps somewhere along the street he collapsed, or found a shop doorway to sleep in, or hobbled into a motel, who knows—he usually found somewhere to sleep the booze of.

Either way, it wasn't important.

What was important, however, was the man who Sullivan had helped, and who'd attempted to help Sullivan in return—and the events this man was about to put in motion.

———

He was positive he'd recognised this stranger, but had no clue where from.

Working for the feds meant you get to know the faces of a lot of scumbags. It wouldn't be the first time he'd walked past a stranger and felt a slight recollection, their face hiding somewhere within his memory. After all, he'd recognised the two guys in the bar—though he knew why he'd recognised them. He was aware of which organisation they were a part of, which was exactly why he didn't want to start anything with them. What would happen when the news reported on a black FBI agent beating up two men in a pub?

Whether or not they were white supremacists, the newspapers would always emphasise the sins committed by a black man.

But this man... The one he'd helped...

He was almost too familiar.

Then he recalled a glimpse.

A mugshot.

Was he a criminal?

Then he realised. He'd watched a program on Fox a few weeks ago. He'd asked his wife to turn it over as the game was on, but she'd said no, as she was engrossed in a true crime show. He generally avoided true crime, not wanting to mix work with pleasure—but this show had intrigued him.

It was called *Most Wanted*, and featured stories on the country's most wanted criminals.

And this man was on it.

"Shit..."

This guy was a hit man. Formerly part of British secret operations, but had since absconded, and continued to commit killings across multiple continents.

He had just helped a serial murderer.

He did not delay—he knew exactly who'd be interested in this case. A colleague who'd gone through the academy at the same time as him—the only other African American in his cohort. As much as things had improved for members of the black community wishing to enrol in the FBI, life in the academy was still not perfect, and they'd stuck together. They'd kept their heads down, supported each other, and made it through twenty weeks of intense training.

This friend's name was Daniel Winstead—and he was not only a dear friend, but he was also a brilliant agent who'd made his way much further up the rankings than he'd been able to.

He put the phone to his ear, told the receiver who he'd seen, and waited to be put through to Daniels' team.

# CHAPTER FIVE

THE COFFEE WAS COLD. WHY WAS THE COFFEE ALWAYS cold? This was the FBI for Christ's sake, the best intelligence agency in the world—they should be able to afford a coffee maker that kept the damn coffee warm.

Special Agent Daniel Winstead poured the black liquid down the sink, resenting seeing good coffee go. He would put the machine on himself, but he didn't know how. It wasn't his area of expertise. He could track trained killers, trace terrorists across the country, and negotiate a hostage situation—yet, as his wife always said, he was unable to make a decent cup of coffee.

Didn't they have an assistant who did this? Wasn't Janine around? Why was she always there when she wasn't needed, yet disappeared when she was?

He leant back against the wall. Closed his eyes. Massaged his temples. Wondered if he'd get to see his kids before they went to bed tonight.

Heck, he knew he should just be grateful. It was hardly easy for a black man to work their way up law enforcement, and he knew he could have ended up like this brother, working night shifts in a warehouse to put his kids through college—but, right now, he didn't care; he just wanted a damn coffee.

Just as he was about to give up, Janine poked her head around the door, her curly hair tied behind her head, a notepad and pen in her hands.

"Daniel, I—"

"Janine, just the person!" He knew she was about to alert him to some crisis—why else would she be here? But, whilst there were always crises to deal with, it seemed there was rarely coffee, and he could really do with a cup. "How do you work this thing?"

He smiled at Janine in a way he hoped was friendly, but feared that he came across as impatient and condescending.

She stepped forward, scooped a few spoons of coffee beans from a packet into the top of the machine, and pressed a button. The machine began making grinding noises. It was that simple.

"Janine, you are a godsend."

"Thank you, Daniel. I just came in here to say that Berkley is looking for you."

"Ah, what is it now?" He rinsed out a cup and stared at the machine, wondering how long it would take to finish.

"They've clocked someone on the most wanted list in New Jersey."

"What? Who?"

"I think his name was Jay Sullivan."

"Jay Sullivan!" Daniel sprung to life, rushing to the door. He told Janine to bring his coffee through when it was ready and ran through the corridors to Berkley's office.

Berkley, a man in his early thirties with a goatee and a poorly fitted suit, sat next to Liam, a man also in his thirties, but with a well-fitted suit. They were like a bad comedy act, these two.

"Berkley," Daniel demanded as he charged in, "what's the status?"

Berkley hit a few buttons on his computer, and an image projected onto the big screen. It was of a man wearing clothes that were once expensive but were now tatty, lying on a bench next to a busy road.

The man looked far from the image of the highly adept, skilful assassin Daniel had imagined.

"Is it definitely him?" Daniel asked.

"Positive face ID," Berkley responded, switching to a window that showed a close-up shot of the CCTV, beside a mugshot of Sullivan, above the words *Face Matched.* "We got a tip off from a former colleague who'd watched Most Wanted on CNN."

Daniel hated television, but right now, he could kiss whoever made that show.

"I don't get it," Liam said. "This guy is ex-British intelligence; why are we so bothered about him?"

"Because he murdered eight US government officials and three civilians on government soil. We've gone almost two decades without a sighting, and now... Yes!" Daniel pumped his fist. "When was this taken?"

"It's a live feed."

"Have we got cops on the way?"

"Yep."

"Tell them to cordon off a 200 metre perimeter and contain him. Unless he moves, do not approach. I want him."

"Wouldn't it be easier to get the cops to apprehend him?"

"The fact that you think the cops would stand a chance at apprehending him shows how little you know about this man."

"He's a drunk sleeping on a bench."

"Trust me." He turned to Liam. "Can you get me a chopper?"

Liam leapt from his seat and out of the room.

Daniel watched their target on the screen as he sat up. Rubbed his hands over his face and through his hair.

"How could he be so stupid?" Daniel wondered.

"What do you mean?"

"He's sitting in full view of CCTV. That doesn't sound right. Could it be a trap?"

"I don't think so. Here's what I found from a few hours earlier."

Berkley brought up a darker clip from during the night. Sullivan staggered against one lamp post, then into a bush, then onto his knees, then pushed himself up again and stumbled further down the street before ending up on the bench.

"He was very drunk," Daniel mused.

"It appears so."

Daniel grinned. He couldn't help it. He gained endless amounts of satisfaction at seeing his enemies being brought down a peg or two. Everyone had feared this man for so many years, and here he was, stupidly drunk to the point that he was unaware that he'd laid down to take a nap right under a camera.

Liam re-entered the room.

"Chopper's ready in ten minutes, they're meeting us on the roof pad."

Daniel nodded. "Let's go."

He went into his office and placed his bullet-proof vest over his shirt, with the letters FBI in bold, yellow letters on its reverse. He placed his Glock 19M in its holster around his belt. By the time he was in the corridor, Berkley and Liam had done the same, and were ready to go.

Liam led the way to the stairs. Daniel took them two at a time without even sweating. His job meant he had to be in peak physical fitness, and that he was—his body moulded in a muscly physique most men hadn't the ambition to acquire, nor the perseverance to attain.

They reached the roof as the helicopter lowered down, his jacket fluttering from the wind of the propellers. He led them aboard.

Berkley informed Daniel that the police were there, and were positioned to contain Sullivan if he tried to leave.

Daniel asked the pilot for their ETA, who responded by telling him it would be approximately twenty minutes.

"Perfect."

# CHAPTER SIX

THE SUNLIGHT PUNCHED SULLIVAN'S FACE.

His nose throbbed. Like it was hurt.

Did someone hit him last night?

He turned his head and groaned. Probably. He imagined, from how antagonistic he could get while he was wasted, that he was probably hit more often than he was aware of.

The sound of cars passed by. The cold of early morning sent a shiver up his body. He was lying on something hard and, as he opened his eyes and squinted, he concluded it was a bench.

He used the back of the bench to pull himself upright and twisted his legs until he was sitting on the bench properly. He felt queasy. His hand flopped to his side and brushed against something lumpy. He turned his head. It was vomit. Brilliant.

He shifted along the bench and away from the puke, as if it gave him plausible deniability that the sick had come from him. A man passed by, looking from the vomit to Sullivan, then averted his eyes upon seeing Sullivan's glare and kept his head down as he shuffled past.

Sullivan focussed on regaining his senses and figuring out

where he was. Slowly, he recalled he was in the US. But how did he get to the US?

He racked his brain. He'd stowed away on a plane. It had been surprisingly easy to do, considering the level of security. He hadn't looked where the plane was going and found himself in... where was he? Was it New Jersey?

He massaged his temples. Tried to keep the memories coming. The US was not an ideal place to be. Not only were they one of several countries who had people dedicated to trying to find him, their surveillance was better than most nations.

He recalled thinking this last night and deciding to stow-away on another plane, but was desperate for a beer before he left. He'd found a bar. And then...

He felt the top of his head. There was a lump. Another injury from another assault, he assumed.

He sat back. Sighed. Ran his hands through his greasy hair. He used to have expensive trims from the world's best barbers; now his scruffy hair resembled a mop head. The suit he was wearing once cost three grand; now it smelt of beer and was covered in stains that even the best dry cleaner couldn't get out.

He rubbed his eyes, picked some gunk out of them, and scanned the street. He was so used to scanning locations and examining civilians it was something he didn't even think about doing anymore; it was important that he checked his surroundings and ensured he hadn't been tracked—especially while he was in a country that would love to capture him.

Cars passed him at a rate of six or seven every ten seconds Most were people carriers with kids in the back. There must be a school nearby. A few expensive cars drove by, driven by men in suits. Either there was a large set of business buildings nearby— which was unlikely as he was in the middle of suburbia—or this was quite a middle- or upper-class estate. Most of the houses on this street had at least four bedrooms. Most probably had swimming pools. He couldn't see a bar nearby, which meant he'd walked at least a few blocks before passing out on the bench.

Most people were too busy to look at him. They probably thought he was a bum, and didn't wish to engage with such a person. Mothers with long, neat hair and sunglasses perched atop their heads push their prams with a bit more eagerness as they passed him. They were the kind of mums who would go on about how important charity was, but would never actually get their perfect nails dirty by helping the needy.

Across the street was a bus stop. An old lady and a teenage boy stood beside it. There were a few local shops nearby. One had CCTV above it. The camera was pointing in Sullivan's direction.

Dammit.

It's okay, he assured himself. There were millions of cameras in this country; neither the FBI nor the CIA could watch every camera at all times. They would only look for him on this camera if they knew he was nearby. Considering he hadn't even been in the country for a full day yet, he was probably fine.

Besides, if he left after staring right into the camera, that would look suspicious. It was best that he took his time.

He suddenly felt parched. He needed water. Or another beer. He reached into his pockets for his wallet.

Gone. Again.

Someone probably stole it. Another reason to despise the human race.

He'd have to go to a safety deposit box and pick up some more cash, maybe a fake passport. Where was the nearest one? He was pretty sure he had one in New York. It had been a while since he'd been in the States, but he knew New York was north of this state.

He leant forward. Covered his face. He really shouldn't have come to the US. How could he be so stupid?

He shook his head.

Was that even a serious question?

He'd had no alcohol for at least five hours before he'd arrived at the airport; of course he would prioritise booze over safety. Even now, he could feel the acidity in his belly and the shakes in his arms that only a few beers could cure.

He closed his eyes and belched. Opened them and squinted. The sun wasn't going anywhere, but it was time he was.

He went to stand up.

Then paused.

Waited.

Listened.

He noticed something.

Everything. It had just...

Stopped.

No cars went by. He peered down the street, looking for distant traffic. Listening for the distant hum of engines.

There were none.

He peered the other way. Listened hard.

There were no people either.

All those parents and their kids were gone. The people at the bus stop had since left on their bus. The busyness of the street had stopped, and it was empty. Deserted.

This didn't feel right.

Sullivan glanced at the camera. Peered at the lens, trying to make out whether it had zoomed in on him, but it was much too far away.

It was as if the area had been cordoned off, and somebody was blocking people from coming down here.

A quick movement in the distance caught his eye. He

didn't see the man clearly, but he was sure they were wearing a bulletproof vest.

"Fuck!"

He stood quickly, not caring about how it looked to the damn camera. Not anymore.

But it was too late.

There were footsteps tapping across the pavement behind him, but he saw nothing when he turned to look.

On a nearby rooftop, a man assembled a sniper rifle.

And from across the street, the wind carried the click of ammunition being loaded into a gun.

He turned and ran.

# CHAPTER SEVEN

"Shit, he's moving. Drive! Go!"

Berkley hit the gas, speeding past the cordons, and racing down the road, following Sullivan as his chaotic limbs carried him down the street. They didn't need to hide their position any longer—Sullivan knew he'd been discovered.

"Target is running," Liam said into his mic, sat in the seat behind them. "In pursuit."

As they approached Sullivan, Daniel had a better look at the infamous man who'd evaded capture for so many years. He felt disappointed. It didn't feel so bad when they thought they were chasing a fit, stealthy assassin—but this person was haggard and downtrodden. He didn't look like an astute, able killer—he looked like a man whom life had swallowed whole then shit out.

Then again, Daniel had been deceived by appearances before—you don't get to his level of rank within the FBI without being aware of everyone's ability to surprise you.

Berkley swung the car in front of Sullivan, mounting the kerb and blocking his escape. Daniel had barely placed his hand on his gun before Sullivan pulled his car door open and flung himself into the front passenger seat with him.

It was a clever move. The closer you are in combat, the harder it is for one to stretch their arm and fire a gun, and the easier it is to be disarmed. Daniel's gun was only just out of its holster when Sullivan grabbed his wrist, twisted it, and aimed the gun at Berkley.

Daniel did all he could to twist his arm and resist Sullivan's pressure, and as Sullivan squeezed Daniel's finger against the trigger, Daniel ensured the bullets landed in the car's roof, rather than in his colleague.

Sullivan twisted Daniel's wrist, straining with sufficient force to make the agent drop his gun, and kicked it under the seat. Sullivan headbutted Daniel, and used Daniel's moment of disorientation to throw his other arm toward Berkley—who had just unholstered his gun—and he entwined their arms together, forcing Berkley's arm to stretch, and for him to drop the gun.

Daniel was taken aback; Sullivan was a contradiction in appearance and ability—he looked like a drunken fool, but his training was so deeply embedded into his instincts that he was still a nimble opponent in hand-to-hand combat.

In the furore, Liam had managed to draw his gun, but was struggling to get a clear shot in the commotion. Noticed Liam, Sullivan flung himself out of the car. Just as Liam opened his car door and went to step out, leading with his gun arm, Sullivan slammed the door against Liam's wrist and forced him to drop the gun. Sullivan grabbed Liam by the collar, dragged him out of the vehicle, then rammed his head against the car's; Liam fell to his knees and struggled to regain balance amid the grogginess.

Sullivan ran away, quicker than the agents could regroup.

Daniel stretched his arm under the seat, but could not reach his gun; he had to step out of the car so he could retrieve it. His outstretched fingers reached the barrel; he pulled it closer, gripped it, then aimed it in the direction in which Sullivan had fled.

As Berkley helped Liam up, Daniel scanned the street.

Sullivan sprinted toward a wall across the street.

Daniel took aim and shot, but only managed to hit the wall as Sullivan's disappeared over it.

He turned to Liam, who'd regathered himself. "Drive around the street, keep close," he instructed.

Liam broke off, returning to the car as Daniel and Berkley ran toward the wall.

"Where are my eyes?" Daniel demanded into his radio. "Talk to me."

The sound of propellers grew louder above him.

"Target is making his way through the gardens," replied helicopter surveillance.

"Roger, we're in pursuit."

Daniel gathered speed, leapt at the wall, and pulled himself up before dropping onto grass, narrowly missing a pond. A woman in a dressing gown stared at them from the glass doors of the house. Daniel opened his jacket to show his badge as he sprinted through the garden. He jumped over a flowerbed, leapt onto the next fence, and dropped into the next garden. He dodged a swing set and a push car as he landed, which threw him off balance, and he'd slipped halfway into a swimming pool before he could grab the side and stop himself from slipping any further.

Berkley helped him up, and Daniel ignored the heavy wetness of his trousers as they continued their pursuit into the next garden.

# CHAPTER EIGHT

SULLIVAN'S BODY FELT LIKE IT WOULD FALL APART AT ANY moment. Every stiff muscle twinged, parts of his thighs that he hadn't stretched in months ached under the pressure, and his hungover mind struggled to keep up. Even so, his instinct still granted him a sufficient level of competence. Years of experience guided him, telling him his next move. He'd chased many people, and he'd run from many people; he'd disarmed many highly trained agents in various countries; and he'd beaten many highly skilled warriors in combat. His government may have brainwashed him and betrayed him, but they had also made a resourceful, adept killer out of him. He was once known as the 'assassin without a gun'—because he didn't need one. He was slick with his hands, and resourceful with his environment. And whilst he may be older, not as fit, and weighed down by an alcoholic's gut, his moves were automatic.

Fighting those men in their own car.

Disarming them.

Fleeing over the fences.

As much as he panted and wheezed, he knew what to do without hesitation.

He leapt onto another fence and pulled himself over, ignoring a splinter in his finger, and landing in another garden. He passed another swimming pool, and more expensive ornaments, and more glass doors leading to fancy kitchens, urging his body across the neatly trimmed lawn and toward the next fence.

The beating of propellers above him, however, told him this would not work. He could escape those pursuing him on foot, but if a helicopter was tracking him, it would make no difference; they could monitor his every move. They'd know where he was going the second he went there. Running through gardens would not help him escape.

So what?

What could he do next?

He could lose the agents in pursuit, but it was hard to lose eyes in the sky.

He tried not to think about his next move, and instead allowed the younger version of his self that lay hidden away, somewhere in his mind, to guide his feet.

If he was still part of the Falcons—the secret government organisation who'd indoctrinated him when he was an impressionable young man—what would he do?

A vehicle.

He needed a vehicle.

That would be a good start.

And he needed to leave these gardens. They weren't getting him anywhere. The fences were slowing him down and making him easier to follow.

He looked over his shoulder as he leapt into the next garden. He could see two men in pursuit a few fences over. He had a head start on them, and had to use those extra seconds to gain some wheels.

He paused in the next garden, picked up a large garden gnome with a quizzical look on its face, and launched the ornament at the glass doors of the house, smashing them. He leapt through the remaining shards of glass as they pricked his calf, and charged through the house.

A woman screamed and backed against the wall. He quickly assessed her: mid-thirties, wearing a pink dressing gown, rollers in her hair. He'd forgotten it was still early morning; time didn't seem to matter much when you don't adhere to set meals or a normal sleeping pattern.

"Where's your car?" Sullivan demanded, stepping over a few Barbies as he approached her.

She just kept screaming.

"I said, where is your car?"

She screamed more, and remained rooted to the spot, her wide eyes fixed on him. She looked to the stairs, no doubt thinking of her daughter.

He glanced over his shoulder. He didn't have time for this.

He put his hand over the woman's mouth and pushed her against the far wall, knocking a few photo frames off a nearby coffee table. He held her in place, muffling her cries, and peered into her eyes with his dead, empty pupils.

"Keys. Now."

She glanced at a bowl on a small table in the hallway.

"Car?"

Her eyes turned to a door behind her. Tears trickled down her cheeks, and he felt bad for the trauma this would cause her.

He released her and said, "Thank you. I'm sorry to have hurt you."

He heard distant shouts of "he's in the house."

Sullivan grabbed the keys and ran through the door the woman had indicated. It led to a garage with boxes lining the walls. Beyond an old barbeque and a broken desk was a motorbike.

He was hoping for a car. He hadn't ridden a bike in a long time.

The woman screamed again. His pursuers were in the house. He didn't have time to deliberate.

He climbed on, kicked away the stand, and turned the ignition. It appeared to be a Honda CB1000R; a beautiful instrument that purred as he revved it.

He rolled the bike forward, and the door opened automatically for him. Bloody rich people.

He accelerated out of the garage and turned to the right. A few bullets landed behind the rear wheel.

Sullivan sped the motorbike up the street, leant to the side, twisted around the next corner, and continued speeding up. The roads were empty, and the bike was fast.

He checked the petrol. It was almost full. He may yet have a fighting chance at escaping.

## CHAPTER NINE

THE SMASHED GLASS DOORS INDICATED TO DANIEL WHERE to go. He stepped over the broken shards into a kitchen, past unfinished colouring books on the dining table and dirty dishes in the sink.

A woman screamed. He feared the worst. He rushed through the hallway, followed by Berkley, and found a woman in a dressing gown, her hands pressed against her wet cheeks.

Daniel produced his FBI badge and said, "Which way did he go?"

"Get out!" she screamed and ran upstairs. She opened a bedroom door, and a child began crying.

This felt wrong. Intrusive. This was a person's home. He shouldn't be in here.

But this was about saving lives. Catching a murderer.

He peered into a living room, looked past a half-built Lego train set and a bookshelf of Disney DVDs. Nothing.

He followed the hallway through, which took him to an open door to the garage. They ran inside and caught sight of a motorbike rolling out of the open door.

"Liam, we need evac now, suspect on motorbike."

"I see him," replied a voice in his ear.

Daniel produced his Glock 19 and fired at the bike, but his bullets ricocheted off the tarmac as Sullivan sped away.

He ran out of the garage and Liam slowed the car down enough for Daniel to climb into the passenger seat and Berkley to climb in behind him. Daniel had barely shut the door as Liam sped in the direction of the motorbike.

They turned a corner, followed the motorbike through the estate, past large suburban houses and picket fences, and onto the highway.

"This is Winstead," Daniel spoke into his comms. "Suspect on motorbike"—he squinted—"a Honda, travelling north on Interstate 95. We are in pursuit, requesting backup."

"That's an affirmative on backup, coming your way now."

Daniel put his seatbelt on and let Liam drive. He wasn't good at giving other people control, and he wished he was driving, but he told himself to trust Liam; high-speed pursuits were his area of expertise.

Even so, he could not relax. This wasn't a regular chase. They'd pursued targets before without him feeling even a slight bit of tension, such is the confidence he had in himself and his team—but this was different. There would be no second chances. If they failed to catch Jay Sullivan today, then he would disappear, and it could be decades until he resurfaced again — if he resurfaced at all.

They had to take this opportunity. It would be the pinnacle of his career.

Liam interweaved between cars, and it only took a few minutes until several police cars had joined them. Their sirens forced people to move over and clear a path in the road, making it easier to pursue their target. In the mirror, he could also see black cars, indicating that his colleagues from the FBI were here.

This was the best chance they would ever get.

Sullivan turned off the interstate and onto Route 9.

Daniel gripped the side of the seat as Liam braked and skidded the car around the corner and off the interstate. He clenched his fists around the leather, terrified they would lose sight of him.

But they didn't. They matched his speed as he raced along the road, allowing Daniel to continue his vehement glare at the murderer speeding in the distance.

The helicopter passed overhead. Even if this many cars failed to catch him, the helicopter wouldn't.

He had nowhere to go.

Daniel wished he could see Sullivan's face right now. He wanted to see what a man like Sullivan looked like when he was scared. He wanted to see how it looked when the uncatchable realised he was about to be caught; how he looked when he realised he would either be left to rot in prison, or sent to die in the electric chair. Personally, Daniel hoped it was the latter—he would enjoy sitting and watching the death of a man who had taken so many American lives.

He checked the speedometer. They were doing well over 100mph. One wrong move, or one simple tap from another car, and they would be dead.

But the risk was worth it.

Out of the window, Daniel could see Sandy Hook Beach in the distance, beyond estates and parks. The bay was the bluest water he'd ever seen.

"Keep going," Daniel urged Liam. "We've almost got him."

———

Sullivan was fucked.

He knew it.

Hell, the FBI knew it. He could imagine them in the cars

behind him, chuckling, watching him in his pointless attempt to flee.

But this was America—and in America, you do everything you can to ensure the authorities do not catch you.

In the UK, they would put him in prison, and he could escape. In the States, he'd be given a death sentence, and there would be no escaping that.

To his right, he could see water. The coast. Beyond suburbia was the bay.

In a move as unexpected to him as to the FBI, he launched himself off Route 9 and toward a set of roadworks. Using the gradient of a pile of rubble, his speed took him over the barrier and onto the roads of a large housing estate.

Several cars braked and honked at him, but he sped past them. He leant far to the side so he could turn quickly around one corner, then around another, taking him closer to the coast.

Over his shoulder, he could see the police and FBI as they were forced to come to a halt; they could not launch themselves over the roadworks, and could do nothing but watch as he accelerated out of sight.

Even so, the helicopter remained above him; the noise of its propellers drowned out by the roar of the bike's engine.

He twisted the bike over a patch of dead grass and toward the beach, where there was a group of young people dressed in scuba gear at the waterfront.

He did not want to scare or hurt anyone else, but this may be his only chance—if they had something he could use to breathe underwater, then perhaps he could stay under long enough for the helicopter to lose sight of him.

He shook his head to himself. How did he get into this mess? And why did he even come to America?

Next time, he'd check where the plane was going before it

took him to one of the few first world countries barbaric enough to still have the death sentence.

Then again, who was he to talk? How many death sentences had he carried out during his time?

He saw them all in his nightmares; the faces of the poor souls he'd taken from their mothers, fathers, husbands, wives and children. He couldn't undo the hits he'd executed when his government had brainwashed him into thinking he was doing the right thing. All he could do was make amends.

And he couldn't make amends if he was dead.

He brought his bike to a halt, ditched it, and sprinted across the grass toward the people in scuba gear.

Above him, the helicopter hovered, and a man onboard brought out a gun.

"Shit," he muttered, and sped up, ignoring the stitch in his side.

They fired their first shot, and Sullivan immediately began his evasion techniques—zigzagging, then abruptly reversing, forcing the shooter to miss him every time. He slowed down as he passed a group of civilians and stayed close to them, knowing the shooter wouldn't risk innocent lives.

Then, finally, he approached the people in scuba gear, scanning their possessions to see if they had what he was after—they had an oxygen tank, a snorkel, and a mask; they just what he needed, already assembled and ready for to take.

He felt bad that he was about to steal it—but the gunfire from above let him off his guilt. With this apparatus, he could stay under the water without having to surface long enough for the helicopter to lose him.

He sprinted harder, ignoring the pain in his legs and his belly and his lungs, grabbed the vest with the oxygen tank, placed it on his back, ignored their protestations, and dove into the water.

Whilst everyone else stepped wearily out of their cars and peered through the barrier like it was a mild inconvenience, Daniel burst out of the car, leapt over the barrier, and sprinted after the motorbike.

He understood why the others weren't doing this—there was no way they would catch a motorbike on foot—but he was sure he knew where Sullivan was going.

The coast.

Sullivan would want to be out of sight of the helicopter— and he could achieve that by using the water.

So he ran across dead grass, past white picket fences, and over freshly mown lawns. He ran past runners, dog-walkers, and men standing on their lawns with a just-delivered newspaper in their hands. He ignored bemused looks from women pushing prams, men in suits getting into their cars, and children walking to the school bus. He entered the park, dodging civilians as he aimed for the narrow path, knocking branches out of his way until he emerged at the other end, running around parked cars as he crossed over the road.

He was fit as hell, goddammit, and he could make it to the coast without so much as a stitch. But if he was honest, as fast and fit as he was, he needed help.

So he paused and spoke into his comm.

"Sullivan is heading toward the waterfront."

"Chopper has visual."

"Take the shot."

"Negative, he evaded the shot, he's too close to civilians."

Daniel punched the air, then kept running as he spoke. "Keep your eyes on target."

"He's entering the water. Looks like he's taken some breathing apparatus."

"When can we get divers?"

"Requesting ETA."

He wiped sweat from his brow. He realised people were staring at him. He met their eyes and they turned away.

"Thirty minutes," said the voice in his ear.

"Thirty? You kidding me? He could be anywhere by then."

"They are mobilising now, sir, there's nothing else–"

"Right, right, whatever."

There was nothing else for it. He was going to have to get there before Sullivan could swim too far. It was a lost cause, but Daniel was a man of lost causes. He managed to get a date with his now-wife after three years of flirting. He had his first child after four years of trying. He rose through the ranks of the FBI despite being a black man with little education.

A lost cause was nothing to him.

So he sprinted, harder and harder, toward the coast, forcing cars to brake and people to jump out of the way. He did not deviate from his course.

But it was no good. By the time he reached the water-front, Sullivan was long gone, and all he found was a group of people in scuba gear bitching about how someone had stolen one of their air tanks.

And if that person was Sullivan, he could stay under the water's surface long enough to be anywhere.

He kicked a nearby garbage can, not caring for the mess he made.

# CHAPTER TEN

SULLIVAN SWAM DEEPER, HOPING THERE WAS ENOUGH oxygen in the tank to keep him going long enough to escape.

He was sure the helicopter was still hovering above the water, searching for him. He was out of sight, but it wasn't enough—he had to keep moving, using the depths of the water to take him somewhere else, somewhere away from the helicopter.

But he hated the water.

The salty water stung his eyes. He closed them long enough to soothe the discomfort, then reopened his eyes to see where he was going.

Not that he'd have any idea.

He could hardly navigate his way to anything whilst twenty feet underwater.

His clothes felt heavy. His muscles ached. Many years ago, he was young, agile, and adept—this would have been nothing. In fact, to even suggest he couldn't swim underwater for long enough to escape would be an insult to his skills and training. Now, his gut felt heavy, and an old scar on his arm was throbbing. It sat just below his shoulder, a decades old mark that he rarely paid attention to—except now, as the salt was mixed with it, and he was surprised to find that it still hurt.

It was one of many scars left by his father, but only one of the few that were visible to anyone else.

His father had been a heroic police officer held in high esteem by the community. He was awarded medals. Admired by his subordinates. Shook hands with the mayor. Prompted other kids to say, "I wish he was my dad."

But behind closed doors, the story was different. Behind the façade, he was an aggressive drunk. A bastard. A man who routinely hit Sullivan's mother, leaving Sullivan to either hide and listen to his mum's anguish, or to stand up for her and face a fierce beating himself.

Then, one day, his father's anger culminated in him killing Sullivan's mother before killing himself. The anger within Sullivan grew a little more intense with each foster home he was transferred to. It seemed that no one was able to deal with him, and he eventually ended up on the streets. That's when the Falcons found him. He was a kid without a reason to live who would be missed by no one—they just needed to give him a purpose, and he would be their willing killer. And that's how the government made him their bitch.

He pushed his arms to the side, dragging himself through the water. His movements were becoming slower and slower as the adrenaline ran out. He needed to preserve energy; he needed to ensure he did not pass out. If he fell unconscious he might float to the surface, prompting someone to call the police – or, even worse, he might die.

Still, he still needed to keep going. He couldn't stop yet. So he kept swimming, slowly, flinching once again at the faint sting of the old wound at the top of his arm.

His father had inflicted this wound on Sullivan a year or

so before his death. Sullivan never understood why he'd received it. Hell, he rarely understood why he received any of his beatings—but this one was particularly hard to comprehend. At least, through child's eyes.

As an adult, he could guess why his father had marked it upon his skin.

He was searching for a place to hide. Dad had come home drunk and was looking for someone to slap with his belt. He resented Mum most at times like this. He didn't understand how she could let him do this to them, and Sullivan hated her for simply withstanding the pain. Sullivan had run through the upstairs hallway, past his own bedroom, which was small and bare, and through to the spare bedroom.

There was a cupboard in this room that was usually locked. Sullivan had never been in it, and he rarely tried to open it as the door wouldn't usually budge. At this moment, however, he pulled at the door, and it swung wide open.

But there wasn't space to hide inside. It was full of all this strange-looking stuff. Multiple items on a thin table draped in a red cloth. Behind them, a flag hung against the cupboard wall—it wasn't a flag Sullivan recognised, though the symbol was familiar.

He'd learnt about it in history class.

They were learning about World War Two, and every time his teacher showed them pictures of the German soldiers, he saw this symbol either around their arms or on their chests.

There were a few items on the red cloth in this shape, such as a thick metal object, and a piece of felt.

There was a framed picture of two S's at the far side of this cloth, both in three thick lines. There was also another framed picture of a shaved-headed man raising his hand like Hitler used to. And a necklace, with a metal pendant that had two words inscribed: *White Power*.

What was this?

"Oi!"

Sullivan spun his head around. He shut the cupboard as quick as he could, but it wasn't quick enough—Dad stood behind him, his police shirt half open.

"What the fuck are you doing?"

Sullivan raised his hands and went to plea, but no words came out.

"Get here, you nosy little shit!"

He grabbed Sullivan's arm and dragged him through the house, down the stairs, and into the kitchen, where he took out a knife.

Sullivan struggled harder when he saw the knife, but Dad was bigger than him, and his dad knew how to fight. It only took a few seconds for Dad to pin Sullivan down on the floor, sitting on his chest and using his spare hand to push down on Sullivan's cheek, flattening his face against the tiles.

That was when Sullivan's father carved the Iron Cross into Sullivan's arm.

Sullivan had a vague recollection of the moment Dad created the wound; he'd felt dizzy, and his arm stung for days afterwards—but there was an image attached to the pain that he couldn't forget. It was his mother, sat at the kitchen table, crying, watching from between her fingers. Terrified, yet doing nothing to stop it.

Sullivan didn't know why he was being punished, but he rarely did. His father was an aggressive man, and the anger he repressed in order to display his perfect image to the community would come back on him and his mum.

Decades later, the wound had faded, and Sullivan found it odd that it had begun hurting again.

After what felt like half an hour in the water, Sullivan was still hesitant to get out, unsure whether he'd made it far enough away—but he was cold, his muscles were burning, and he wasn't sure how much oxygen was left in the tank; he had no choice but to take the risk. He swam upwards and, as his head rose above the surface, he relished an intake of clean air.

Across the water, he could see the outline of the tall buildings of New York. He swam toward them.

# CHAPTER ELEVEN

WITH HIS HANDS ON HIS HIPS, FOOT TAPPING, AND LIP twitching, Daniel watched as his team searched pointlessly for Jay Sullivan.

The divers arrived when he was told they would, but they all knew it was too late. They found nothing.

The helicopter hovered over the water, scanning for a figure moving beneath the surface. After all, how deep could Sullivan had gone?

Nothing.

And the rest of the agents and officers stood at the coast, looking pathetic. Standing around, waiting for Daniel to give them further instructions. But there was nothing they could do until they had a confirmed sighting, and he was too enraged to look at them.

Berkley took a statement from the civilians in the scuba gear, but what the hell was that going to do?

This was ridiculous.

They'd had him. They had eyes in the sky and *how many* people chasing him? It had been almost impossible to lose him.

Yet they had.

Of course they had.

Sullivan had evaded capture from several countries for several years. He existed in a world where he was impervious to the law. He believed he didn't have to answer to his crimes. And he had the skills to evade capture, despite the odds being so insurmountably against him.

Daniel kicked a bag of equipment, emphasising his frustration with a loud, "Fuck!" He didn't know whose bag it was, and he didn't care. Whoever it belonged to, they were incompetent anyway, and they could clear up the damn mess.

He wandered away from his team massaging his temples. He just needed a minute. A bit of time to calm his temper.

Sullivan hadn't escaped yet. He had to believe that.

They had just lost sight of him temporarily, that was all.

So what next?

If the divers and the helicopter find nothing—which Daniel was sure would be the case—they needed a next move.

Where could Sullivan go?

He would have to re-emerge on land at some time—the oxygen tank would last an hour at most—and he would have to re-join the coastal path when he did.

Unless he commandeered a boat.

Those were the two possibilities, and Daniel had to counter both of them.

"Liam," he demanded, and Liam ran up to him. "Get a unit to search every boat up and down the coast for at least five miles."

"Don't we need a warrant for that?"

"Does it look like I give a shit about a warrant?"

Liam nodded and said, "Affirmative." He took his phone out and stepped away.

"Berkley?"

Berkley marched to his side.

"I want a presence along the coast," he instructed. "Police, FBI, whoever we have—I want them to station themselves every 200 metres along the coast, in both directions, watching for when he gets out of the water."

"I don't know if we have enough–"

"Then find enough!"

Berkley nodded, then took out his phone and scuttled away. Each car left, following Berkley's orders of where to station themselves.

Daniel rubbed his head. It was pounding. He was thirsty. And he hadn't had enough coffee.

Once Berkley and Liam confirmed that Daniel's instructions were carried out, they reappeared at Daniel's side.

"Drive me up the coast," he told them. "We'll keep searching, back and forth. He's got to resurface at some point."

Without a word, they obeyed his command. Daniel sat in the passenger seat, searching every face they passed, and peering at the coast, hoping to catch sight of a downtrodden has-been trudging away from the water's edge, his clothes drenched.

He would not give up. Jay Sullivan was somewhere close, and he was going to find him.

# CHAPTER TWELVE

WALTER OFTEN WATCHED WELL-DRESSED FAMILIES FROM HIS barstool as they sat around a table in the restaurant section of the pub. He would observe the way they smiled at each other like they were putting on a play, and he would think... that could have been him.

To Walter, the school his parents had worked hard to get him into was just another form of prison. They had repeatedly forced him to revise, desperate for him to pass an entrance exam to a prestigious academy—but school was never the right place for him. He despised being told what to do, and would often sit in class, wondering what gave the teacher the right to decide when he could sit, or stand, or talk, or stay silent—or even go to the toilet. Society? Well, fuck society. He'd never chosen this world; it had been chosen for him.

He'd truanted many of the lessons, and he'd often be kicked out of the ones he showed up to. It took only four months since starting at the school for them to exclude him permanently.

Then Mum and Dad were able to convince a local private

school that Walter was not a lost cause. He was brighter than other sixteen-year-olds; he could increase their average grades and make the school look better. His parents were such good talkers that they negotiated a 70% discount on tuition fees through some kind of scholarship for intelligent but misinformed youths. It still cost them a lot—Mum had to take an extra job, and Dad had to work more night shifts—but they did it without hesitation.

Walter was kicked out of that institution on the day before his fifteenth birthday.

He simply wasn't interested in *their* version of education. There was nothing they could teach him, apart from how to conform to their propaganda. They preached cultural tolerance. They preached helping inferior races. Their history lessons were full of lies. And whenever he'd ask to move seats as he was too near the black kid, they would shove *their* rhetoric down his throat. Walter had already been mixing with white supremacy groups for years, and he knew more than the school could ever teach him—in fact, he believed he should be the one teaching *them*.

At first, the groups were about identity. He was used to being a loner; the smart kid who made everyone else look bad. Then a group of lads with shaved heads and bomber jackets stood up for him when the Hispanic group of kids tried to beat him up in the toilets for beating their test scores. From then on, he had somewhere he belonged.

That was when he met Curtis, who had already been excluded from four schools, and was going to a remedial school to finish his final exams. He didn't show up to any of them; he was too busy with Walter, following *White Knights* around Europe—their favourite white supremacy metal band.

His parents kicked him out when he turned eighteen. He'd kept his jeep parked outside the house with a swastika painted on the rear and *White Power* written on the sides, and his parents gave him the ultimatum: either the jeep goes, or Walter goes.

He left the next morning.

And now, here he was, five years later, in a two-bedroom flat behind the railway lines. Dirty plates with pizza crusts sat on the floor beside empty beer cans. He and Curtis's beds were unmade; they were too busy playing *Call of Duty* online, always taking the side of the Nazis, only going outside to visit the pub or to cash their welfare check. He hadn't spoken to his parents in all this time. He'd received Christmas cards, but that was it. They usually contained a long letter about what they were doing and how they hoped he was happy. He never sent one back.

He had more important things to do.

He was leader of the US division of *White Avengers*, and there was pressure on him to guide the group in the right direction. The German sect had already burnt a synagogue to the ground, and the Polish sect had beaten a homeless black man to death.

But what the hell were they doing?

At the moment, his division looked weak. They had done too little to be recognised. No blood had been shed, and other sects were wondering if he was the best leader to guide them. He was full of inaction; what difference was he making?

Well, if they had given him his passport, he could have performed his planned attack in the UK—in fact, at that very moment, the television displayed a news reporter who was reminding him why he had chosen the UK as a target.

"Curtis!" he called.

Curtis came out of the kitchen, wearing nothing but three-quarter length blue jeans and his Doc Martens. "What?"

"Look at this."

The news reporter was discussing how Syrian asylum

seekers were arriving in the UK. After fleeing the war-torn country on boats and crossing the oceans, they landed on British soil, and some of them were even given jobs. He'd thought that Brexit meant the UK would reject immigrants, and he'd been proud that the US had such a close relationship with them—but now, here the UK was, welcoming foreigners in like old friends.

"Fucking sick," Walter growled and threw his empty beer bottle at the television. It hit the table the television stood upon, then fell on the floor beside a pile of open DVD cases with missing DVDs.

"Bunch of wetback-loving bastards," Curtis said.

"Fucking immigrant scum and hippy loving bullshit."

"We ought to kill the whole fucking lot of them."

"Fucking-a."

But Walter was not allowed a passport, as they had informed him that morning. He considered, for a moment, whether he could sneak aboard a boat, or a plane, but they did not have the financial resources to achieve such a difficult task—besides, that's how the asylum seekers sneaked their way over.

"Wish there was a way," Walter mumbled.

Curtis grinned. He pointed at Walter, an idea clearly emerging, and began jigging back and forth, giddy with possibilities.

"What?"

Curtis sniggered, flexing the eagle tattoo on his bicep, wrinkling the SS beside his eyes.

"What is it?"

"We might not be able to bomb them in their country—but what if we don't need to?"

"What do you mean?"

"I mean the fucking embassy, man—it's not that far."

"Won't an embassy be armed to shit?"

"Dunno. But we have enough of us and enough guns that we can shoot them all before they even look at us."

"But they'll shoot back—"

"So some of us might die for the cause, so what?"

Curtis was right.

He was crazy, but right.

The embassy...

It was bigger than beating on a homeless man. It was even bigger than a cheap bit of arson. It would show all those other sects who was the most militant, the most powerful, the most serious members of the alliance—it would put his name on the map.

"We'll need even more guns," he said. "And lots of them."

Curtis's grin spread wider across his pale face. "I can get us more guns."

"How soon could we do it? A month? Maybe even a few weeks?"

"Nah, man, they have people. The FBI and the cops, they see us getting guns and shit, they'll track our messages, our social media, and they'll know. We need to do it quick, before they pick up on it."

"Then when?"

"How about today?"

"Today? We need time to get our shit together."

"You just need to get everyone armed and there. We send out a message now, people will respond. They are all waiting, Walter, and they are waiting for you." Curtis crouched in front of his leader, patted his cheeks and salivated with anticipation. "You give the call, everyone will follow. Believe me."

Walter went to object, then didn't.

Could they really mobilise within hours?

He couldn't. But Curtis...

There was little that Curtis couldn't do.

"Do it," Walter said.

Curtis pumped his fist into the air and screamed out in celebration, hooting and whistling and dancing and jumping.

"Heil Hitler, brother," Curtis said.

"Heil Hitler."

He shoved his gun down the back of his trousers and danced out of the apartment, leaving Walter alone to contain his excitement.

# NEW YORK, US

# CHAPTER THIRTEEN

SULLIVAN EMERGED FROM THE WATER, SHIVERING, hobbling toward the city scape. As he hid himself among the buildings, past run-down pharmacies and fast-food shops covered in graffiti, his dislike of humanity was reinforced by the way strangers turned away from him. Not that he wanted attention—quite the opposite—but it was still so typical of people to ignore a man in need. He was clearly in a bad state, and people avoided looking at him rather than offering help.

Back when he worked for the Falcons, he'd go into hiding following a hit—at least until the uproar had passed—and he would often spend that time in the British countryside, in cottages surrounded by fields, or bed and breakfasts along an endless country path. If he went to a local village looking like this, in that kind of place, people would talk to him; they'd be concerned, and make sure he was okay. But here, on the coast of Brooklyn, humanity's true side became apparent. He was like the rats that scuttled past one's feet; people would rather not look down to see what they were stepping over.

A glossy-yellow school bus passed, and he lifted his collar to avoid the stares. Patches of dead grass adorned small lawns outside small homes. People sat on porches talking about nothing and everything. He was satisfied that he'd passed them unnoticed—then he passed a police car.

Two men in uniforms leant against the bonnet, coffee-to-go in their hands, sharing a conversation about sports. Sullivan reckoned there'd be several police cars stationed along the coast, searching for a likeness to his photo. But police weren't invested in this like the FBI, and evidently weren't as attentive, meaning he was able to put his head down and cross the road undetected.

Still, CCTV cameras could track his movements. It wouldn't take much to identify a drenched guy of his stature walking through the city. He needed to look less conspicuous —and that started with drying off his clothes.

He located the nearest public toilet and entered, greeted immediately by the rancid stench of piss, and two men who abruptly stopped what they were doing to glare at him. Their hoods were up. Faced toward each other. Exchanging something between them.

Sullivan nodded at them and walked to the sink. He put the hot tap on and ran his hands beneath it. The heat was painful, but it was a relief when compared to how cold his damp clothes had made him.

"Yo, cracker," one of the men said. He sounded like he belonged to a gang in a Hollywood film.

Why did everyone in America sound like they are from a movie?

Sullivan looked at the man in the mirror. "Yes?"

"Don't know if you can tell, but we're in the middle of some shit here. How about you wait outside?"

"I'm quite all right leaving you to do what you need to do, if you leave me to do what I need to do."

He meant it. He had no interest in an angry drug dealer. If anything, he was doing these guys a favour—if a cop came into the bathroom, they would be more likely to arrest Sullivan than a gangbanger dealing a bit of weed.

"I don't think you heard me," the man said, turning toward Sullivan, trying to make himself look taller. "I said get out."

Sullivan forced a smile. Oh, how he wanted to be left alone.

"No," he said, quiet but forceful.

The man chuckled in a way he clearly intended to be sadistic. He produced a gun and pointed it at Sullivan. He held it horizontally, a clear sign of an amateur. If he fired that gun, it would break his wrist.

"Get the fuck out before I pop you."

"Before you pop me?" Sullivan tried not to snigger.

"You heard me."

Sullivan was wet. He was tired. He was fed up. He was not in the mood for this.

"Yo, I just told you to get the fuck out—"

Sullivan grabbed the guy's wrist and twisted it. It forced the idiot to his knees and loosened his grip on the gun, allowing Sullivan to snatch it away.

Sullivan didn't like guns. They were loud and messy. But he'd seen enough to recognise that this was a Glock. He released the magazine with his thumb and allowed it to drop to his other hand, then pulled the slide back slightly, and turned down the slide lock to take it apart. He dumped the pieces in the bin and turned to the drug dealer with his eyebrows raised.

"Now *you* get the fuck out." Sullivan said. The dealer and druggie scampered out of the bathroom like prey fleeing a predator.

Finally alone, he removed his jacket and his t-shirt first. He avoided looking at his scarred skin in the mirror as he held the items under the hand dryer. After a few minutes, he put them back on, then did the same with his trousers. This didn't make his clothes particularly dry, but they were less wet; waiting until they were fully dry would take too long. He needed to leave the city, and he needed to do it quickly.

Did he have any contacts in New York? He thought about it. None that he could recall. Perhaps he could get to the airport. How far was it?

He needed a map.

He opened the door, went to leave the toilets, then came to a halt as he almost bumped into someone entering the public toilet. His attention was immediately drawn to the stranger's uniform.

It was a cop.

He held the door open for them.The cop smiled at him and made his way into a cubicle.

Sullivan stayed inside the public toilet and shut the door. The cop might not recognise him, but when he sees his picture again, it might prompt his memory, and they will know where to concentrate their search. The area would be flooded with cops and FBI before he knew it.

The only decision now was whether to hurry out and run, or whether to knock the cop out once he'd finished his shit.

## CHAPTER FOURTEEN

THE FIRST, AND MOST IMPORTANT THING TO DO IS TO remove any panic from your mind and your body.

And that was what Sullivan did. He relaxed the muscles he could feel tensing, calmed his breathing, and stopped his thoughts from racing ahead of him.

He stayed by the door, listening to the cubicle lock, the unbuckling of the belt, the sigh as the police officer sat down, and the flatulence as he began emptying his bowels.

The cop had walked in with the same arrogant swagger Sullivan had seen in cops before, and he struggled to control his rage—it reminded him of his father. It was the same strut his dad would enter the house with after a long day of playing the hero. He'd remove his belt, then hold it aloft like a trophy before dropping it on the kitchen table. He'd unbutton a few buttons on his shirt, look at himself in the mirror, and you could almost see him thinking *I am one fantastic son of a bitch*.

This would normally precede the drinking and the beatings—the moments where he revealed the self-contempt he concealed beneath the authoritative stride. He'd stay in his police uniform for as long as he could; he loved feeling like he was worth something. It was a persona Sullivan did not want his father to drop, because that's when the self-loathing would reduce him to violence.

Sometimes, his mates would come around and drink beer in front of the television, watching the football, or the boxing, or whatever sport would allow them to channel their aggression for the evening. Sullivan would sit on the landing, watching his mother lying on the bed between a crack in their bedroom door whilst listening to his dad's conversations. His mother would use this time to rest, and wouldn't dare show her face downstairs, fearful of the ridicule and chauvinistic comments and dogged leering she would receive.

He remembered one occasion, when his father was showing off to his friends about an arrest he'd made.

"It was another one of those black kids—you know, the ones that hang around in the alley?"

"Fucking scumbags is what they are."

"He marched out to me with his jeans sagging beneath his boxers, you know, the way they all do."

"Does my fucking nut in."

"And he gets in my face and says, what you gonna do about it, piggy?"

"Piece of shit."

"And I tell him that if he or his mates talk to me like that again, I'll break his jaw."

"Good on you!"

"And do you know what the prick did?"

"What?"

"Told me to go back to sizzling in the frying pan."

"I don't get it."

"A joke about smelling bacon, being a pig, something like that."

"What a fucking idiot."

"So I say, boy, you just fucked with the wrong policeman.

You should have seen him when his parents came to get him from the station the next morning. They were furious he'd gotten himself arrested. They were saying shit to him, like how they'd taught him to be careful with cops, not to give them an excuse. See, that's the problem, isn't it? They tell their kids the cops hate them, then they get aggressive toward us, and we have no choice but to be dicks back."

"That's the thing about blacks—they are all so fucking angry."

"And if they just stuck to their own neighbourhood and kept the crime out of ours, maybe they wouldn't need to be so careful around us."

As he recalled this conversation, Sullivan listened to the cop ripping off pieces of toilet paper and felt a fluttering of hatred toward this officer.

This was decades later; maybe attitudes weren't as bad. But Sullivan recognised the walk. He recognised the attitude. The arrogance. He knew he was making an assumption, but he couldn't help making it.

"Officers, we have sighting on Sullivan."

It was the officer's radio.

Sullivan's eyes widened, and he listened carefully.

"This is Daniel Winstead of the FBI."

Sullivan logged the name—*Daniel Winstead*. He must be the man leading the search.

"CCTV has picked Jay Sullivan up on Coney Island, walking east up Nautilus Avenue. He is noticeably wet, wearing a black suit in poor condition."

Sullivan couldn't wait any longer. They were closing in on him, and he had to move.

He dumped the suit jacket in the bin, opened the door, peered down the street, and walked out.

# CHAPTER FIFTEEN

SULLIVAN TURNED LEFT DOWN NEPTUNE AVENUE, CROSSING the road on the thick intermittent white lines, not wanting to be hassled for jay walking.

He kept his head down, but his eyes up. He passed a young couple with their lips attached to each other and took a hoodie the boy had draped over the back of the bench without being noticed. As he put it on and lifted the hood, he noticed some sunglasses and caps displayed outside a newsagent. Wearing both would make him look suspicious, so he just took a cap, placed it under his hood and atop his moist hair, and kept on walking.

He passed a run-down liquor store to his left that provided an aroma Sullivan was all-too familiar with. It smelt like cheap hotel rooms and troubled mornings. An old man prompted a chime above the door as he left with two paper bags of liquid comfort. Sullivan resisted the temptation to join him and walked on.

A black car came to a stop outside a grocer at the end of the seat. Three men in suits stepped out. They couldn't be more obvious if they tried. Sullivan turned away from them, down West 15<sup>th</sup> Street, passing a gated home and a long line of parked vans.

Shutters concealed garages. Graffitied signs marked the territory of local gangs. Youths with nothing better to do than stand around street corners, intimidating passers-by. Then a man with a sun visor, polo shirt and white shorts strode toward him. He was a Caucasian man, dressed like a Caucasian man, in a predominantly black neighbourhood. It was too obvious. Sullivan turned toward a dumpster, pretending to put something in it as he turned his back to the man.

He was about to change direction to avoid a confrontation—then he changed his mind. The city was full of cops and agents. They knew he was in Brooklyn. They would track him. He was going to struggle to escape, and he needed to know where they were in order to find a route where he could avoid them, and this obvious agent could give him that information.

So he turned and followed the man dressed like an out-of-place tourist down the street.

As he did, he inspected the man further.

Sullivan could be wrong. The guy could be a genuine civilian, wandering around his neighbourhood.

But guys like that don't live in a neighbourhood like this.

He was wearing cheap trainers. Too cheap. As if intentionally cheap. Over thick sports socks with *Fitness For Us* logo on them. Memberships to that gym were easily $70 a month. The guy didn't belong here. And, as if that wasn't enough, there was a bulge in the back of the guy's shorts where a gun looked to be concealed. A man like this wouldn't carry a gun in this kind of neighbourhood unless he was looking for trouble.

Sullivan quickened his pace.

They approached a side street.

Just as they did, Sullivan grabbed the guy's head and knocked it against the wall. As he checked no one was looking, he shoved the guy to the filthy pavement of the side street, taking the gun from behind this man's shorts as he did.

He mounted the man and placed the end of the gun against his forehead.

"Please! Please! Don't hurt me!"

It was a convincing performance.

"Please, I only carry the gun to protect myself, I don't want to hurt anyone!"

"How many of you are there?"

"How many? I'm on my own."

Sullivan sighed. This guy was going to keep up the performance for as long as he was able.

"You see my face?" Sullivan said, keeping his voice low. "You know who I am?"

The man stared up at him, fear gripping his eyes, and did not respond.

"I'll take that as a yes," Sullivan concluded. "In which case, you know what I can do, and what I have done. So you know I will kill you, don't you?"

The man hesitated, then reluctantly nodded.

"So how many of you are there?"

"I don't know. I was just told to walk down this street and scan for—"

"Right, okay, okay."

This guy knew nothing.

Sullivan held the gun back and struck the barrel into the man's forehead, knocking him out. He took the gun apart and placed it in a nearby dumpster, then knelt beside the guy's head and turned him on his side. He found what he was looking for inside the man's ear.

A tiny earpiece that he placed in his own.

"CCTV outside a liquor store has him on Neptune Avenue."

"Roger, heading there now."

Sullivan dragged the unconscious body behind the dumpster and stepped back into the street, waiting, listening.

"Heading north on West 15th Street."

That was this street. He needed to move.

He turned to the left and walked as quickly as he could without running.

"I have eyes on him. Wait to confirm."

Dammit.

Sullivan ran.

"Target is running."

Sullivan sprinted.

"Pearson is down, behind a dumpster."

"Stay in pursuit."

Sullivan sprinted harder until he came to a dead end.

# CHAPTER SIXTEEN

DAMMIT.

How could he be so stupid?

He was better than this.

Well, he used to be better than this. Had he lost that much of his former self?

In a way, that was a good thing; it meant he was no longer a killer. Still, he needed to keep an element of ruthlessness to escape such situations.

Right. Just stop. Concentrate. *Think.*

To his right was a fence. Over that fence were diggers and mounds of dirt and stone.

He grabbed hold of the top of the fence, pressed the bottom of his feet against it, and dragged himself upwards. He rolled over the top and fell, landing on his back, a familiar ache in his spine.

"Davidson has eyes on target, he's mounted a fence."

He had no time to lie around and wait for pain to subside. He shot to his feet. Sprinted—at least, he ran in what felt like a sprint with his aching legs—climbed up the digger, leapt onto a nearby wall, and jumped onto the bonnet of a car.

"Target has leapt over the wall and is now on Stillwell Avenue."

He looked to his left. To his right. Ahead of him was the edge of a bridge that led to more water. He'd had enough of water.

He turned left and ran.

"Heading north on Stillwell Avenue."

Sullivan came to a halt. Looked up at the sun. What time of the day was it? He was fairly sure it was close to midday. By that logic, he was running south; right toward them. So he turned and ran the other way, past shutters and run-down car-sales stores, and fences covered in graffitied bubble writing.

"This is Purvis. Target in sight."

He looked over his shoulder. A car approached; black, with shaded windows. Not even bothering to look inconspicuous.

He turned and ran at the car, not sure what he was doing. The car slowed down, he slid over the bonnet, opened the car door, and punched the driver in the face before he could withdraw his gun.

He pulled the man out of the car but, before he could get in and commandeer the vehicle, a gunshot ricocheted off its roof.

Sullivan ducked down, using the car as shelter.

The man groaned and turned, opening his eyes.

Sullivan grabbed him with one hand, removed his gun with the other, and placed the pistol against the back of his skull. He stood, shielding himself with his hostage.

Another car had pulled up; two men threw themselves out and pointed their weapons at him.

He recognised them. They were the two blokes who'd pursued him through the gardens. The one on the left was evidently in charge.

"Drop it! Drop it now!"

Sullivan didn't want to kill his hostage. He was probably an honest person, following orders, trying to keep food on the table for his children. Maybe he had a wife. And a mother. And a father.

Sullivan never used to care if his targets had a wife or mother or father, he'd kill them anyway—now, the families of the people he'd killed were all he could think about as he lay awake at night, and he desperately didn't want to add another face to his nightmares.

"Don't come any closer!" Sullivan instructed.

They stopped walking, and edged forward instead.

"I said stop!"

"Just put the gun down, Sullivan! It's over!"

To hell it was.

He backed up to a nearby fence covered in black graffiti that concealed a small house. Took a deep breath. Shot at the ground a few steps from the feet of his pursuers, forcing them to retreat, and used their momentary panic to shove his hostage to the floor and leap over the fence.

He took the gun apart as he made his way across an overgrown lawn, leaving pieces of artillery strewn across a flower bed of wilting stems. He twisted the door handle, relieved to find it open, and strode into the house. A black man almost twice the size of Sullivan rose out of a seat in the living room, leaving his daytime television to confront his home invader.

"Who the fuck are you?"

Sullivan didn't stay to fight. He ran through the house, looking for a garden to enter.

But there was no garden. There wasn't even a backdoor. Just a wall painted blue and marked with stains.

Sullivan turned to the large man, whose body lurched toward Sullivan, fists clenched.

"Please," Sullivan said, raising his hands. "I'm being chased by the FBI. They are out to get me. I need..."

What did he need?

Rather, what on earth could this man do for him?

There was one way in or out. There were three FBI agents waiting for him, and now there were probably more.

The man reached into a nearby drawer and produced a gun.

Sullivan huffed. Why did everyone in America have a bloody gun?

Sullivan kept his hands raised. "I'm not here to hurt you. You know what the authorities are like—they shoot first, ask questions later."

"That may be," the man replied. "But you can't stay here."

"But I—"

"I want to help you, brother. But my daughter sleeps here. She will be home from school in a few hours. I don't want any trouble. Whatever shit you got with the cops, that's your shit, not mine, and I think you need to leave."

Sullivan admired the man. So calm, so rational. Like people here often encountered others who were running from the law. In a place like this, the authorities were just another gang.

But the man was also right. Sullivan could not bring his trouble to the house of a father. It was not this stranger's fight.

"Jay Sullivan," came a voice through a megaphone from outside. "Come out, we have you surrounded."

The stranger cocked his gun.

"Okay," Sullivan said. "Okay, I'm leaving."

His mind raced with what he could do next; how he could keep evading capture. Unfortunately, no ideas came to mind.

Oh, how happy these bastards will be to have caught the great Jay Sullivan. This will be the defining moment of their career. Someday, they will tell this story to their grandchildren. They will become legends in the academies.

And Sullivan will rot on death row.

He stepped forward, retracing his route through the house, aware of the man's gun following his every movement.

Sullivan paused by the door. Looked back. Noticed a drawing on the fridge; a little girl and a large man, with scribbled lines and dodgy colouring in. It made him smile.

His daughter used to draw him pictures like that, once upon a time.

He nodded at the stranger. Turned the handle. Opened the door. Trudged across the large blades of grass to the gate and beheld the sight.

Cops. FBI. With their bullet-proof vests and marked and unmarked cars, arranged in a semi-circle across the street. Ten, possibly twenty, men stood, pointing their guns at him.

"My name is Daniel Winstead," said the man who had chased him previously. He was a well-dressed African American with confident determination in his voice. "And you are under arrest. You need to do everything we say, or we will shoot you. Do you understand?"

Sullivan nodded vaguely, then scanned the faces of the men aiming their instruments of death in his direction. Even now, as fucked as he was, he was still scrutinising possible escape routes.

Could he go back over the fence?

Get beyond them and jump over the bridge?

Could he fight all of them?

The answer was no to all the above. No one was close enough to fight, and there was no way he could run without being shot; each person was eager to be the one who took him down, and if he moved even a few inches, they would open fire.

"I need you to answer us audibly, Sullivan. Do you understand?"

A sigh. "Yes."

"Now put your hands in the air."

It was humiliating. They loved every minute. The sons of bitches.

He put his hands in the air.

"Now get on your knees."

"Are we really doing this?"

"I said get on your fucking knees!"

Another sigh. This one longer. Exasperated. He was coming around to the notion that he had no escape, but had not yet adjusted to being part of this tired ritual.

"Now!"

Sullivan slowly lowered himself to his knees.

"Now lay down on your front."

"I'm not lying down."

"Do it!"

"I am not lying down."

"Do it, or we will shoot you!"

He huffed through gritted teeth. His arms tensed. His legs shook. His entire body seized with wounded pride, his ego shot to pieces.

He lay down on his front.

"Keep your hands on your head."

Daniel holstered his gun and approached Sullivan, his handcuffs out.

Sullivan had no choice but to accept being handcuffed. They were tight, and it hurt, and he struggled to balance as Daniel dragged him to his feet and hissed into his ear, "You are fucked now."

Daniel shoved him in the back of a car.

Sullivan kicked the driver's seat and let out a large roar, furious with himself for being so stupid, wishing he hadn't been so reckless.

Daniel climbed into the seat next to him, and his two colleagues climbed into the front. As they drove away,

Sullivan met Daniel's eyes—he'd never seen someone look so smug. He felt his body fill with hate, and he looked forward to the day he could show this guy exactly what he thought of him.

For now, however, he was caught, and it appeared that Daniel had won.

# CHAPTER SEVENTEEN

AN ARTIFICIAL AMBER LIGHT FLICKERED AGAINST THE bathroom's white tiles. Mould lived between each tile, crusted black residue surrounding the edges of pale plates.

Walter looked in the mirror. Its corners peeled. He couldn't remember ever looking into this mirror without smudges causing a distortion of his features. But today, he didn't care. He had lived in squalor because he couldn't get a job. He'd been told in several interviews that he wasn't the 'right person'—but he knew it was really because they'd rather save money by employing immigrants.

But today, that was going to change.

Today, he stood against all those fake whites who betrayed their own kind by favouring a weaker race.

Today, he stood against all those Jews who ran the country in secret and pretended not to crave power.

Today, he stood against all those negros and spicks who ever made him feel unsafe to walk down the streets in his own hometown.

They'd shout. They'd holler. They'd bump fists and bump

shoulders like they were proud of each other; like it was okay to be who they were.

Today, he would show them it wasn't okay.

And so he dressed. A plain white t-shirt. Light blue jeans attached to braces that he fixed over his shoulders.

His hair was barely a centimetre thick, but to him, even a shred of hair wasn't acceptable. He squirted a blob of shaving gel on his hands and spread it over his head. After washing the remnants of gel from between his fingers, he took his razor to his scalp and used light strokes to avoid bleeding. He'd done this many times, and he was good at it. He loved the feel of the blade on his head, the roughness of the edges, and the process of rinsing the blade, then starting again.

Once he was done, he ran his hand over his skull, feeling the tiny pricks of hair barely visible in his reflection.

He flexed his muscles, showing off his bare arms and the ink he'd so proudly had engraved upon him. Any sign that represented the cause was there: swastika, Celtic cross, iron eagle, 88, 777, agliz, Arian nations sword, blood drop KKK— and his favourite, the skinhead Jesus hanging off a crucifix on his shoulder.

He lifted the gun he'd placed on the back of the toilet when he'd entered. Felt the weight of it. Thought of the power he held in his hand. It was the power to choose who lived and who died.

And he thought of Curtis.

Sometimes he wondered if Curtis loved the cause, or just loved chaos. He was standing in the living room, waiting for Walter, more loyal than anyone he'd ever known.

At the age of fifteen, a group of Hispanic boys had shoved Walter around for beating them on a maths test. Really, they didn't give a shit about the test—they were looking for an excuse. Curtis had bitten one of them on the neck. He'd head-butted another. And with the final one, he'd placed the fucker's mouth on the curb and kicked hard against his skull.

They expelled Curtis for it, but Curtis didn't care. School wasn't for him. They'd remained best friends ever since—and it was in the year that followed that incident when Curtis taught Walter his greatest lessons, and introduced him to the people who'd become his inspirations.

And now he was waiting to be Walter's right-hand man in the greatest moments of their lives.

As was Herman. And Simon. And Corey. All five of them had gathered, armed themselves, and agreed that, if they had to go down in flames, it was for a worthy cause.

It was for their race, and for their country, and ensuring the two were mutually exclusive.

But the embassy wasn't the final part of that plan, and that had been Curtis's suggestion—and what a beautiful suggestion it had been. They had far greater intentions than a few hostages in a building. Once they had finished causing death and destruction in the embassy, and ensured the listening world knew their cause, they would create an effigy in the streets outside the White House...

It would be iconic. A perfect moment in history. A sign to those who hide their beliefs because of a misguided society that oppresses them for knowing the truth. This story would be told to generations of white kids, and they would hail Walter as a hero.

It would show other sects and factions and groups that it was time to join them in the ultimate race war—where the whites were sure to come out victorious.

They may lose people, but Walter had come to terms with that. So long as he and Curtis set this world on fire, he'd be proud to have fought for his cause.

A teacher once told him—if you stand for nothing, you'll fall for anything.

The same teacher was shocked when he heard what Walter believed, which was a shame, as that man had taught Walter his greatest lesson. But Walter didn't allow such fools to deter him.

With this thought spurring him on, he stood tall, puffed out his chest, and left the bathroom.

Curtis leant against the kitchen counter, twirling a gun in his hand and holding a half-empty beer bottle in the other. He grinned as he watched his companion enter the room, appreciating the confidence in Walter's stride.

"Yeah!" he screamed, raising his fist into the air.

Herman, Simon and Corey all followed, raising fists, screaming in solidarity, adrenaline surging them toward their goal.

"Are we ready?" Walter asked.

"Fucking-a!" Curtis confirmed. He downed his beer then straightened his back, his braces holding his jeans up over his bare chest. His eyes, his skin, everything about him would strike terror in their enemies.

"Let's go fucking do this!"

With roars of confirmation, Walter led his group to the car.

# CHAPTER EIGHTEEN

As Sullivan sat in the back of the car with nowhere to run—for now—he was able to study his opponent more carefully.

Daniel Winstead stared back at him with a mixture of awe and satisfaction. This was the pinnacle of this man's career, and he looked smug about it. The glare above his pristine suit summarised everything Sullivan hated about the FBI: the arrogance, the black and white view of society, and the belief that anyone they catch is filth.

"Are you going to stare at me for the entire journey?" Sullivan asked. "I know I'm pretty, but I'm not that pretty."

Daniel snorted and turned to the window. He sat with his legs wide apart like his crotch was a grand artefact to display. Sullivan imagined he was the kind of guy who drank protein shakes every morning, went to the gym like it was his religion, and saluted the flag with pride.

Sullivan's father would have hated Daniel: he despised proud black men. Someone who celebrates how far he's come despite the obstacles against him. To Sullivan, this was probably the only thing he admired about the man. His father, however, would assert that "the proud blacks" were "the worst kind of blacks."

"They all seem to think they deserve to share the same air as us," he remembered his father saying one evening, as his younger self eavesdropped on his father's conversation with his drinking pals. "They should be grateful we've let them live."

Sullivan bowed his head. Sometimes he wondered if he had any good memories of his father, and he would spend lost afternoons and empty evenings trying to find one.

"So how does it feel?" Daniel asked, not looking at Sullivan, but gazing out the window as he rested his chin on his fist. He was so cocky. Sullivan hated him with a passion that burned inside of him, a glower of rage that made his arms shake — or was that because of lack of booze?—but it was not just the guy's arrogance Sullivan despised; it was how this arrogance reminded Sullivan of himself. And there was nothing he disliked in a person more than similarities to himself.

Sullivan didn't answer. He waited for the man to turn and face him. When Daniel finally turned to face him, Sullivan held his glare, feeling the power imbalance between them; neither of them were able to concede their dominance over the other. Every interaction with Daniel felt like an argument over who had the bigger dick.

"I said, how does it feel?"

"How does what feel?"

"To be caught."

"Is that what I am? Caught?"

"I don't see handcuffs on anyone else."

"You think this is the first time I've been in handcuffs?"

"I think this is the first time you've been this fucked."

"You'd be surprised."

Sullivan mirrored Daniel's blank expression. Barely blinking. Eventually, Sullivan felt a half smile grow in the corner of his mouth. This guy's desperation to maintain authority was amusing. As much as he tried to straighten and stiffen his body, his fingers still drummed against his tie, a nervous fidget that Sullivan couldn't help but notice. Daniel evidently didn't realise who he was fucking with.

"But I bet–"

"Do you know how many people I've killed?" Sullivan leant toward Daniel, grinning harder at the man's refusal to flinch, and kept his voice low. "Did they tell you that in my file?"

"I'm not interested in–"

"Do you know what they put me through when they were training me? About how they tortured me for weeks so I'd know how to handle being captured? I was waterboarded, stripped, electrocuted, starved, deprived of sleep..."

"You are not–"

"And you think that you, a little man in a big suit, sitting there trying to mind-fuck me, is going to get one over on me?"

Daniel said nothing. Sullivan enjoyed the silence; it was an ambitious FBI agent's feeble attempt to cling onto the last bit of authority he had over his prisoner. Sullivan relished it. Let it fester like a sick odour Daniel couldn't get enough of.

"I'm not scared of you," Daniel eventually asserted.

"Aren't you?"

"No. You have a beer gut. You're unfit. Your reactions are slow. Whatever they taught you has clearly gone."

"Why don't you take me out of the handcuffs if you're so sure? We could both step out of the car see how much of my training I remember?"

Sullivan turned to indicate his bound hands, and looked over his shoulder at Daniel.

"Go on," he urged. "Let's play."

Daniel didn't flinch.

Sullivan waited.

Still, Daniel didn't bite.

Eventually, Sullivan turned back around and grinned.

"I thought so."

Daniel went to speak, but didn't.

"I am a British citizen, you know. I have a right to be extradited."

Daniel snorted. "We aren't giving you up."

"Aw, that's sweet."

Daniel huffed. He turned to Sullivan, and he finally bit. "And do you know why we aren't giving you up?"

"Because of my charming personality?"

"No. Because we have something the British don't. Do you know what that is?"

"Wide-spread obesity?"

Daniel leant toward Sullivan and whispered, "The death penalty."

And there it was. Sullivan's fate laid out before him. He would be locked up and put to death.

He refused to let it phase him. He willed himself to hatch a plan. Something cunning. Something that would see his escape.

Buildings passed, and they looked vaguely familiar. It didn't take long until Sullivan recognised where he was. They were near New York's British embassy. He'd been there a few times before, often to reunite with the Falcons after a hit.

What if he went to the embassy now? What if he gave himself up to the British? They would refuse to let the Americans have him and, without the death penalty, he would still have hope of escape. Hell, he'd escaped a British prison before.

The only problem? Getting away from three armed FBI

agents with his hands bound behind his back. Not something easy to do in his situation.

But not impossible.

He'd been trained to make a weapon out of anything, and with this in mind, he scanned the car for possibilities. A pen in Daniel's pocket. A bottle in the back of the chair. And a seatbelt that Daniel wasn't wearing.

*A seatbelt...*

It was perfect.

But he had to think this through. He had to get this right. He needed to make Daniel annoyed, so he was upset. Reckless. Easy to beat.

"Do you think you're better trained than the Falcons?" Sullivan asked.

"Yes."

"The people who trained me? Do you even have clearance to know who the Falcons are?"

Daniel didn't respond. He bit his lip and turned his gaze away. Calmness was power, and Daniel was doing all he could to cling onto that. It made Sullivan chuckle.

"Would you like to know how many FBI agents my government had me assassinate?" he asked.

Daniel's face flickered—just for a brief second—and Sullivan saw the fear he was after. He saw the child inside. The scared boy. The idiot masquerading as a leader. He saw the wimp who didn't want to die; whose patriotic beliefs would only go so far until he broke under torture.

Sullivan said nothing more. He just grinned, sat back, and watched the city go by, satisfied that Daniel was uncomfortably on edge.

The British Embassy was just around the corner. It was time.

# CHAPTER NINETEEN

IN. OUT. IN. OUT

Sullivan calmed his breathing.

He wasn't as agile as he used to be, but he could still beat these idiots.

He flexed his hands. The handcuffs behind his back were frustrating, but he'd overcome worse.

He prepared himself for the move. It would have to be quick. Nimble. Ruthless. And he would have to get it right first time.

He counted down. Preparing himself.

Three.

Two.

One.

In a move too quick for Daniel to register, Sullivan turned his back to Daniel and grabbed his seatbelt with his bound hands. He stretched his arms out, wrapped the seatbelt around Daniel's neck, and pulled hard on the seatbelt as Daniel gasped for air.

Daniel instinctively took his gun out—just as Sullivan had hoped he would. Sullivan kicked it out of his hands, sending it to the floor of the car, and swung his body behind Daniel—so that by the time Liam had slammed on the brakes, and Berkley had turned around and aimed his gun, Sullivan had Daniel between them, suffocating and unable to talk.

"Drop it," Sullivan instructed.

Berkley didn't.

Sullivan pulled even tighter on the seatbelt. Daniel was going red. He was probably trying to tell Berkey to just shoot, but couldn't speak. He tried elbowing Sullivan, so Sullivan wrapped his legs around Daniel's torso to restrict movement of his arms.

Berkley lowered his weapon.

"Out the window."

Berkley huffed, wound down the window, and threw the gun outside.

"You too."

Liam wound down his window and threw his gun outside as well.

"You," Sullivan directed at Berkley. "Get the keys from his pocket. Put them on the seat."

Berkley reached toward his boss and took the handcuff keys from his pocket, then placed them beside Daniel's squirming body.

"Open the door," he told Daniel, and Daniel did as he was told.

Sullivan let Daniel go, grabbed the keys and the gun, and ran.

He could hear them rushing out of their car as he sprinted around the street corner. Unlocking the cuffs while running was tricky, but he managed it. He made it past the embassy entrance and down a side street, searching for a way in that meant he needn't delay his entry by going through the security checks.

He found a window, smashed it, climbed in, and dropped

to the floor. He stood to find a gun pointed at him, and he quickly aimed his gun back.

He was in a security office, and the man aiming the gun in his direction was a lone security guard. There were security jackets in a cupboard behind the guard, and a desk behind Sullivan.

"Drop the gun," the guard instructed, but Sullivan could hear the shaking in his voice. The man was slightly overweight, a few years older than Sullivan, and could be easily beaten.

"I don't want to hurt you," Sullivan said. "Please, just let me in."

The security guard did not yield.

————

"He's going for the embassy," Daniel said, rubbing his neck. Even though it was no longer being squeezed, it still felt tight.

He took another gun from the car boot and sprinted around the street corner, the others following.

The British Embassy was on an ordinary street next to offices and expensive flat blocks. The embassy itself looked inconspicuous, like it could be any building. It had three stories, with several windows and a fire escape.

"This way," Daniel barked, approaching the security and showing his badge. "Special Agent Daniel Winstead."

The security person nodded and opened the door. The opening hallway was grand, with pristine black-and-white tiles on the floor, and marble arches holding up the domed roof. Daniel's shoes made squeaking noises as he entered.

As they approached the front security desk, a man with a metal detector approached.

"Empty your pockets," he instructed.

"We don't have time, we need to—"

"You are not coming in unless you empty your pockets."

Daniel huffed and did as he was told, went through the metal detectors, then collected his gun and his badge.

As sneaky as it was, he did not want the British to know they had Jay Sullivan in the building, for fear that they would not give him up—the UK wished to try Sullivan just as much as the Americans did, possibly even more considering it was their country that he'd turned against.

They had to find him.

## CHAPTER TWENTY

THE CAR'S ENGINE SCREAMED EVEN LOUDER THAN THE white-metal band bursting out of the speakers.

Walter didn't care. Such material items were meaningless. He saw black guys driving around in their fancy cars; it didn't reflect good taste, only how society favoured the wrong people.

Curtis swung the car around another corner. For a moment, Walter thought he was going to run a red light—the last thing he wanted was to get pulled over before they even reached the embassy—but Curtis brought the car to a screeching halt.

Walter turned the music off.

"We have five minutes to go," he said. "Let's not attract attention."

"Right you are, boss," Curtis said. The inflections of his voice came across as manic, and to anyone else, he might seem unhinged—but to Walter, he was just Curtis.

Mental. Scary. Fucked-up.

But not unhinged.

His anarchy was too organised and well-thought out to ever be unhinged.

The lights changed, and Curtis drove the last five minutes of the journey with nothing but the rattling of the engine to calm their nerves. Walter glanced at the expressions of his comrades on the backseats, and he could see his focus reflected.

They reached the embassy and parked a few metres from the entrance

An armed man stood outside the doors.

Walter took a moment. He felt the pride. Felt the justice. Foresaw the events that were about to take place. Kept himself calm as he prepared for a successful mission.

It was a beautiful day.

In a final act of solidarity, he turned to his comrades and held out a fist.

"White pride," he said, and all five of them placed their fists together and repeated, "white pride."

"Curtis," Walter said. "If you will."

"With pleasure."

Curtis stepped out of the car and paused. Sized up the security man. Stretched his bony arms and bared his skewed teeth. Once he was ready, he sauntered toward the security man like a madman doing a poor job of acting nonchalant.

Immediately, Walter could see the look of bemusement on the security man's face. The man's grip on his gun tightened, and he watched Curtis with a morbid fascination. Curtis said a few words to the security personnel. They engaged in conversation, like they were discussing the weather, and the security guard relaxed his grip on the gun.

Then, in a movement so quick the man could not react, Curtis's withdrew a blade from his belt and swiped it across his man's throat.

That was Walter's cue.

He took out his AK-47, ensured the gun was loaded and that the safety catch was off. He picked up a large crowbar, placed the bag of guns and ammo over his back, then turned to see the others with their guns and their bags ready. They burst out of the car and sprinted toward the embassy, joining Curtis, who plunged the blade into the man's neck, over and over, until blood had overtaken the stranger's face.

"Come on," Walter urged Curtis.

Curtis, evidently enjoying his work, begrudgingly stopped stabbing the man, straightened his back, and kicked open the door to the embassy.

Walter, Herman, Simon and Corey burst in and, before the men with the metal detectors could react, aimed a stream of bullets in their direction.

By the time their magazines were empty, their targets were lying stationary on the floor. Walter placed the crowbar through the door handles of the entrance and, as they reloaded their guns, he moved forward to admire the destruction.

Empty faces with wide mouths stared up at them.

Walter had never killed a man before, and he expected to feel more. Remorse, maybe. Hesitation, perhaps.

As it was, he only felt justice.

Yes, their victims were white—but anyone who fraternised with their enemy was as evil as their enemy, and they deserved their death.

As Walter's hearing readjusted following the cacophony of bullets, he realised the receptionist was screaming.

"Curtis?"

Curtis leapt onto the receptionist's desk, grabbed her by the collar, pulled her over, and shoved her to the floor. He licked his lips as her dress rose up her legs. He pulled her to her feet and shoved her at Walter, who grabbed the back of her neck and put a gun to her head.

"Don't move," he told her.

They had their first hostage. How exciting.

Curtis charged into the room behind the receptionist and forced another group of people out. All office workers, none of them armed, eight men and women.

Now they had more hostages.

This meant they had plenty of collateral.

Curtis shoved them all to the floor and told them to stay still. They did as he said. Some put hands on their heads, most stared at the marble surface, and a few even wept. One or two started praying. Another kept muttering about how he had a daughter. Curtis kicked him in the ribs and told him to shut up.

Soon, Walter would tell Curtis and his men to sweep through every room, to kill anyone that opposes them, and to disarm anyone who is subservient and take them as a hostage. Outside interference wouldn't take long, but Walter was confident no one would try to enter the building so long as they had hostages.

But first, they would wait.

People will have heard the bullets and would soon come running; they had to take out all the people who wished to be heroes first.

# CHAPTER TWENTY-ONE

It was a simple moment. It lasted seconds. Though it felt far, far longer.

As the moment began, Daniel was amid conversation with Berkley and Liam. They were discussing strategy. How to look in the various rooms without arousing suspicion.

Then the gunshots began.

Before he'd even consciously acknowledged himself doing it, Daniel had pulled his gun out, and he was running, and his colleagues were with him. At first, he thought it was Sullivan —then he realised there was more than one shooter, and he doubted anyone would be crazy enough to help him.

He didn't even stop to think how crazy it was that they were the only people who would run *toward* the gunshots. Apart from a few other members of security personnel who had appeared behind them, most people were fleeing, or hiding under desks and behind chairs.

He did not acknowledge that he was running, with his gun out, toward gunfire, until the gunfire was so loud that every shot made his head throb, and he looked down to see his feet moving.

For most people, their instinct would be to run from danger. Not Daniel. His instinct was to save lives.

Two of the more inexperienced members of security ran out of the hallway and into the reception area without thinking of slowing down. Daniel watched their bodies spasm as bullets made impact with their chest, then they fell heavily to the floor.

He skidded to a halt and took cover in the corridor, just next to the large open entrance to the reception area. He did not know what they were dealing with. Who these people were. How armed they were, how skilled, and how many. He needed to assess the situation before he engaged.

He waited. And then the shots stopped.

A tense silence hung in the air, the reverberations of gunfire still ringing in his ears.

"We know you're there," came a voice. A man's. Low-pitched and calm.

Daniel pushed himself against the wall. Sweating. Trying to keep his racing mind focussed. Trying not to let the adrenaline push him into reckless action.

"We know there are three of you."

Daniel looked at the others. How did they know that?

"We have hostages. A lot of them. I have my gun against the receptionist's head, and my friends have guns aimed at all the other little office workers. We have already killed today, and we are ready to kill more. Do you understand that?"

Daniel closed his eyes. Urged himself to think. Find a solution, and quickly.

But it seemed as if surrender might be the only option. For now, at least.

If they allowed him to surrender, that is.

"I just asked you a question. Unless you want us to start shooting hostages, I suggest you–"

"Yes!" Daniel shouted. "Yes, I understand!"

"Then you will each step out from behind the wall, place your gun on the floor, and put your hands on top of your head."

Daniel looked at the other two. They stared back at him, waiting for instructions. He was the senior agent. He was the one they expected to come up with a magic answer. Yet he'd never felt like he knew less.

"Three seconds until we kill a hostage. Three. Two."

"All right, all right!"

Daniel stepped out from behind the wall, holding his hands above his head, his gun dangling from his forefinger.

He nodded at the other two, and they did the same.

To his left, a man emerged from the shadows with an AK-47 aimed at him. A man who must have been watching them from the darkness, unnoticed—a man who could have seen from his position that there were three of them.

And a man who looked delighted at the sight of Daniel.

Although *man* would be a loose term—he didn't look much like a man. Every part of his flesh was covered in ink. His eyes were tattooed black. He looked more like a monster than a human being.

Then Daniel noticed the tattoos on his body. The swastikas. The Arian alliance. And he realised what he was up against, and how much these people would enjoy having a hostage like him.

"Drop the guns."

Daniel turned to the man giving the instructions. He was wearing braces, a white t-shirt, blue jeans, had similar tattoos down his arms, and was aiming his AK-47 at Daniel.

Daniel counted three more of them. They stood around a large group of hostages who were crouched on the floor. Some were whimpering. Most were shaking. Every one of them was terrified.

Daniel dropped his gun, as did Liam and Berkley.

"Curtis, if you will."

The monstrous looking man—Curtis, it would seem—walked over and took their Glocks. He tucked one down the back of his trousers and threw the others to his friends. Their eyes lit up like children opening presents on Christmas.

Curtis frisked each of them. When he found Daniel's FBI badge, he showed it to the one who'd spoken to them, and they seemed to become giddy. Then Curtis stepped back and kept his gun aimed at their heads.

"All yours, Walter," Curtis said.

"The two behind you," the man giving instructions said to Daniel. It appeared his name was Walter. "They can come and join the hostages."

Daniel turned to Liam and Berkley and gave them a faint, reluctant nod. They joined the hostages on the floor, staring at him like two children on their first day of school. It's strange how they could reduce three tough FBI agents to vulnerable wrecks with just a little overpowering. He reminded himself that they were human, hoping it would quell the shame.

"What now, Walter?" Daniel asked, emphasising his name. He needed to be on personal terms if he was going to manage any kind of negotiation.

Then again, these men didn't look like they were here to negotiate.

"What now?" Walter mused, licking his lips. "What now... What now..."

Walter stepped toward Daniel—but instead of going around the hostages, he went through them, stepping over one, then the other, not caring whose fingers he crunched, each of them cowering as he passed.

"You're in control," Daniel said. "What happens next is your decision."

In his periphery, Daniel noticed Liam doing something.

Readying himself. Looking around. He'd found something, and he was clutching it in his hand—a letter opener, perhaps.

Daniel beseeched Liam in his mind to do nothing. To just obey. But it wasn't in their instincts.

Walter stepped over the final hostage and moseyed toward Daniel, looking him up and down, surveying him as you would a hog you were about to spit roast.

Liam leapt to his feet and launched himself across the room, aiming the letter opener at Daniel's neck. He was only a few metres away, but it made no difference. Curtis fired his gun. Liam's body flopped. Hostages screamed. A pool of blood spread across the solid floor from Liam's head.

Daniel didn't quite realise what had just happened.

Walter looked over his shoulder. Liam's face was wide-eyed and empty. Walter nodded at Curtis; a sign of gratitude for saving him.

And Daniel realised his colleague was dead.

"What did you do?" he cried.

"It isn't what we've done," Walter said, moving to within inches of Daniel. "It's what we're going to do."

Walter's grin widened.

Before Daniel could respond, Walter instructed Curtis to move through each of the three floors. "Ensure compliance. Round up all hostages. Kill anyone who doesn't cooperate."

Curtis nodded, and two of the men followed him down the corridor.

Daniel shook his head. "So that's what this is about? You don't like black people? And I'm going to be the one you make an example of? That it?"

Walter sighed, stuck his bottom lip out, and nodded.

"Well, look at you!" Walter slapped Daniel playfully on the cheek. "You must be one of the smarter ones."

# CHAPTER TWENTY-TWO

THE SOUND WAS UNMISTAKABLE.

Gunshots. Lots of them.

Sullivan and the security guard exchanged concerned looks, despite the standoff they found themselves in. Sullivan imagined that the guard would believe the gunshots were to do with him.

In fact, Sullivan had no idea who they might be, and the gunshots were a huge concern. The FBI would hardly shoot up the embassy to get to him, so who could it be?

"I need to see who's doing the shooting," Sullivan said.

"Don't you move," the guard responded.

"They are nothing to do with me."

"Yeah. Sure."

Sullivan huffed. This guard evidently felt quite highly of himself, but in truth, he was just a huge inconvenience.

Sullivan sidestepped toward the door.

"I said don't move."

"Give it a rest."

Sullivan opened the door ever so slightly. There were men further down the corridor. He tried to identify who they were, running through all the possibilities: Islamic extremists, professional assassins, protestors. These people didn't look like any of them.

"Get away from the door!" the guard demanded.

Sullivan closed the door. Turned to the guard. Sighed. "I can help you."

"Shut up!"

"Honestly, I am probably the safest person to be in a room with right now, we need to—"

"I said shut up!"

Sullivan made a bold decision. An act he hoped would show this man he wasn't the enemy. He lowered his gun and tucked it behind his waist.

"I'm not going to hurt you."

The guard looked confused. He went to say something, but before the conversation could continue, the door handle turned.

It remained locked.

Sullivan glanced at the window he'd climbed in through.

"We need to go."

"No. You're staying right here."

"I'm leaving. You can come with me if you wish."

"No!"

The door shook. Someone was barging against it.

"You can't do this without my help."

Gunshots. The door lock trembled.

He couldn't wait any longer.

He leapt onto the desk, then climbed onto the window ledge.

"Come on!" Sullivan said to the guard, then threw himself out of the window.

He waited in the side street for the guard to join him.

The guard didn't.

But the sounds were unmistakable:

The door barged open. The guard shouted something. Gunshots were followed by a slamming on the floor.

Silence lingered, then heavy footsteps marched away.

Sullivan waited a little longer, until it was safe, then climbed back through the window. The guard was laid on his back with a bloody hole in his forehead.

He bowed his head. Closed his eyes. "Fuck's sake..."

Why couldn't the man have listened?

Sullivan raised his gun. Waited for the shooter to come back.

They didn't.

Then gunshots came from the next room, then the next, gradually decreasing in volume as the attacker continued down the corridor.

———

The security guard fell to the floor, colliding with the desk. The gun felt hot in Curtis's hand. He paused for a moment, reminiscing about how he'd held this gun in his right hand as he fucked a woman over the bonnet of her husband's car last week, recalling how powerful it made him feel.

Fuck, he loved to fuck.

Then he readjusted his focus—*concentrate, Curtis*—and he left the empty room.

He kicked open the next door and fired his gun, as he did with every room, hoping to shoot anyone who attempted to shoot him the instant the door opened. As it was, there were only two helpless women in this room, both screaming from beneath a desk. Curtis nodded at Herman, who stepped in and grabbed them, shoving them toward Simon, who dragged them into the main hallway to join the other hostages, then returned to Curtis so that they could continue to the next room.

And this was how they continued throughout the corridor.

His Doc Marten boots slamming against the door—after shooting the lock if it wouldn't open—followed by a few bullets aimed inside the room. Then he'd wait to see if anyone retaliated. If he so much as thought someone had a gun in their hand—or anything that looked like a gun— he executed them. Simon and Herman would then take any hostages to the reception area, and Curtis would try the next room.

It didn't take long before blood decorated most of the rooms. Curtis tried to keep count of his tally. He'd beaten the shit out of many, many people throughout his life—he'd even shot at a bunch of blacks who stepped into his neighbourhood—but killing was a new sensation, and he wanted a total to brag about later.

By the time they'd finished on the ground floor, he'd counted five. Give or take. Three dicks and two bitches.

It made him giddy. He practically danced from room to room, light on his feet, like a possum or a fairy spreading their bloody joy.

As they reached the stairs—two more floors to go—he reloaded his gun and turned back to his comrades.

Their faces were so serious. This was a job for them. They were focussed, and they were ready to do what they must.

But this wasn't a job for Curtis.

It was foreplay.

It was a playground.

It was theatre.

He led them up the stairs and onto the next floor, where a few guys with guns waited for them behind the cover of open doors.

"Oh, boy, a gunfight!" Curtis declared in his best imitation of a cowboy.

The other two hid in the stairwell and tried to be strategic.

Curtis thought, *fuck that*.

He marched through the corridor, his gun held high, and sprayed bullets everywhere he saw movement.

It didn't take long before anyone who might oppose them was dead.

———

Sullivan waited for the gunshots to become fainter. By the sound of it, they were going upstairs.

Once he was sure they were on the floor above, he slid out from beneath the table and stared at the open door.

And he waited to be wrong.

But the gunfire was growing distant.

He pocketed the guard's keys, not knowing if any of them might help. Holding the gun by his side, he tiptoed to the doorway and peered down the corridor. To his right, he could make out the feet of some hostages. He did not know what the situation in that room was, and he was not about to enter a battle that he knew little about, so he turned to his left, and edged along the corridor, stepping over a few more bodies, passing open doors and empty rooms.

By the time he'd made it to the stairwell, there wasn't any distant gunfire.

Still, he did not relax.

He entered the stairwell, aiming the gun ahead, then aiming it upwards. He ran up the stairs until he reached the door to the next floor and peered through its window.

There was no movement.

He leant against the door, nudging it open, slowly, and crept into the corridor.

He did not find any attackers. They had evidently finished

making their way through this corridor. What he did find, however, was devastation and destruction; bodies lying limply on the floor; splashes of blood over previously pristine walls; doors with locks shot to pieces and tables upturned.

Some bodies had guns on them. Most didn't. Most were civilians working in the offices. They must have been terrified. And now they were another statistic.

He wondered what might have convinced someone to hurt so many innocent people; what cause they thought they were fighting for. Then he quelled the thought, willing himself to focus, and passed each door with his gun ready, hoping he would not need to use it, but holding it high just in case.

After a while, he grew weary of looking at rooms of death, and he stopped. He'd seen enough.

Whoever it was who'd taken over this building, they were armed, and they meant business.

Even so, it all seemed so... reckless. Like they had a plan, but no organisation.

Sullivan came across the CCTV room. He entered, locked the door behind him, and placed his gun on the table. A body dressed in a security uniform leant against the middle screen. A line of blood trickled down the screen above the corpse's head.

Sullivan moved the body aside and let it drop to the floor, then took his seat at the monitors.

He watched a few men return to the reception area on the ground floor. He counted five terrorists in total. Each of them were skinheads. He peered closer at the screen and noticed a few swastika tattoos.

They were white supremacists. Bloody hell. As if there weren't enough foreign terrorists to contend with, now these pricks were shooting up their own country.

They kept a group of hostages on their knees, heads on

the ground. Sullivan reckoned there were about forty of them.

Which meant forty lives could still be saved.

There was one hostage, however, who was not on the floor. He stood against the wall with his hands on his head.

Daniel Winstead. FBI agent. The man who'd arrested Sullivan.

An African American.

"Jesus..."

If they were white supremacists, why hadn't they killed him yet?

The answer was simple. Sullivan had dealt with enough scum to know how their minds worked.

It was because they had a plan for Daniel. They had chosen him. He would certainly die, but probably in the most disgusting, violent, and public of ways. They would make an example of him. He was to be used as a demonstration of their cause.

Sullivan sat back. Sighed. This wasn't his fight. He shouldn't even be here. He could use these monitors to find a way out of the building. He could escape and not have to deal with it.

But what if he could help?

He ran his hands through his hair. Drummed his fingers on the desk. Glanced to the floor, then back at the monitor. There were five terrorists. Fortyish hostages.

He had expertise that could come in useful.

But fuck it, why should he? Why was it always up to him to help people who wouldn't look his way if they passed him in the street? Who would walk on by, not wanting Sullivan to be part of their world?

The government had people who could handle this situation. He could leave it up to them.

Besides, if he got involved, Sullivan would probably just

wreck any chance there was of saving lives. He had a tendency to fuck everything up. Just look at his life. At his daughter. All perfect examples of what happened when Sullivan tried to do the right thing.

He wasn't meant to be here.

This was *not* his fight.

And it was probably best if he was to leave.

# CHAPTER TWENTY-THREE

THE DAY HAD STARTED OUT SO PERFECTLY.

Daniel had woken up before his alarm. By the time he'd showered, his wife had made waffles. He'd dropped the kids off at school, watching them fist bump their friends, then driven into work. Somebody had left cake in the break room to celebrate a birthday. It was banana cake—his favourite.

Then he'd heard that they had a sighting of Jay Sullivan. Then they'd caught him; the most elusive target they'd ever pursued. Then they'd lost him. And now Liam was dead. Lying a few feet away from the hostages.

And with the gunshots they'd heard from the floors above, and the few hostages they had brought down, Daniel wondered how many more bodies were left upstairs...

These people were in control. There was no doubt about it.

Daniel didn't like relinquishing control, but he had no choice. And, whilst the terrorists didn't appear to be professionals, what they lacked in skill, they made up with insanity.

"Can I ask a question?" Daniel said, without realising he was saying it. He regretted opening his mouth, then he changed his mind; if these people were going to die, they deserved to know what for.

The one they called Walter paused an in-depth discussion with one of the other terrorists and turned toward Daniel.

"It speaks," Walter said, then let the insult hang in the air.

Daniel looked around the hostages on the floor, face down, whimpering and shaking, staying quiet, a few silently praying to a god who wasn't listening. Meanwhile, Daniel was standing against the wall, away from the other hostages, his hands in the air and his legs aching from not being allowed to move.

"I just wanted to know why I am having to stand up?" Daniel said. "Why am I not on the floor with the rest of the hostages?"

Walter leant against the reception desk and smirked at Daniel, chewing gum with his mouth wipe open.

"You want to sit down?" Walter asked. "Next thing we know, you'll be asking for a bathroom break."

"In all honesty, that was going to be my next question."

"If you need to go, then just go. We won't judge."

"You want me to piss myself?"

"I want you to shut up and stand there like a good little slave."

"Is that what this is about? My skin colour?"

Walter pushed himself off the counter and sauntered toward Daniel with a deliberate, arrogant swagger to his stride, like he was trying to impersonate the bad guys he'd watched in all the America-fuck-yeah action movies.

"This is about *our* country," Walter said, his voice losing its sadistic playfulness, replaced with a rising aggression. "This is about *you* taking it from *us*. I mean, you're a special agent in the FBI. You know an American could have had that job?"

"I am an American."

Walter shook his head. "Your ancestors weren't."

"It's *your* ancestors that brought my ancestors to America."

"For slaves. Not as equals."

"We're not equals."

"Finally, you've got something right."

"We are far from equals. I am so much better than you."

Walter strode forward and swung the end of his AK-47 into Daniel's forehead, knocking him to the ground.

"Get up," Walter instructed.

Daniel didn't.

"I said, get up!"

Walter pulled Daniel up and struck him with the gun again. A cut formed on Daniel's forehead. Walter pulled him up once more and struck him a third time.

Then he didn't bother pulling Daniel up. He struck him over and over, and Daniel could only cover his head and wait for the outburst to end.

Finally, Walter stood back and spat on his prisoner—raining thick phlegm upon Daniel.

"You do not speak unless spoken to. Do you understand me, boy?"

Walter wiped Daniel's blood off the grip of his gun and onto his sleeve.

"I said, do you understand?"

Daniel looked up at Walter, angry, his pride wounded, hoping against hope that he'd eventually see this man get his comeuppance.

"You better answer me," Walter said, then placed the end of his gun against Daniel's cheek.

Daniel wiped a hand across his forehead, smudging blood across his face, then looked at the red stain it left on his fingers.

"Crystal clear," he said.

"Now get up." Walter pulled Daniel to his feet. "And shut the fuck up."

Walter strutted back toward his comrades, all of whom were sniggering. They congratulated Walter as he returned to their side.

Moments later, Curtis marched in. Flickers of blood painted his skin, but he wore it like a medal.

"Done?" Walter asked.

"All clear," Curtis confirmed. "Have you checked outside?"

"No, why?"

"There's like twenty FBI agents and cops around the entrance."

Walter echoed Curtis's sadistic grin. "That didn't take long. Should we do something?"

"Nah. Look at how many hostages we have. They wouldn't risk coming in. Let them waste their time negotiating." Curtis looked over his shoulder at Daniel and added, "When the time comes, we have what we need."

# CHAPTER TWENTY-FOUR

THE LIVE FEED FROM THE CAMERA FIXED TO THE OUTSIDE wall was displayed on the monitor. On it, Sullivan could see the exterior of the building. The authorities had cordoned the street off. The building was surrounded by police cars, and black cars with blacked-out windows. People in bullet-proof vests with FBI written in bold yellow surrounded the entrance, along with a few cops. They all had guns.

Sullivan rolled his eyes. Of course they did. This was America. Even the local baker probably had a bloody gun.

Despite there being so many cops and agents, none of them were entering. Which was sensible. They did not know how many hostages there were. They could not risk life. Fairly soon, Sullivan imagined a trained hostage negotiator would ring the reception phone and try to find out this information. They would speak calmly, listen, pretend to care, and pretend to sympathise. They would go through the FBI rule book step by step.

Sullivan had seen it enough times.

He had also seen it fail enough times.

His only concern was how long the authorities would

leave it before entering. For example, what if the terrorists didn't respond to negotiation? What other move did they have?

Surely the FBI wouldn't enter...

Sullivan had witnessed the authorities making stupid decisions before, and he knew he needed to intervene to ensure they knew what they were dealing with; so they knew how many hostages' lives would be risked if they tried to enter.

He searched the body beside his feet for a mobile phone. Found one. Used the man's thumb to unlock it. Searched for the FBI website, found a general phone number, and rang it.

As he was put on hold, he scanned the FBI agents outside the building, searching for something that he could use to prove he was actually there.

Eventually, a woman answered, tired and uncaring.

"Hi, I am one of the hostages in The British Embassy. I need to speak to whoever is in charge."

"Okay, sir, and what did you say your name is?"

"I didn't."

This woman didn't sound interested. She wouldn't. They probably had many calls like this. So he interrupted her insistence that she took his name.

"Listen, I am inside the building, looking out at the FBI. There are..." He counted. "Five FBI cars, three police vehicles. A man with dark blond hair is talking to a man in an Armani suit. That man has a small goatee. Three of the FBI agents are women. Is this enough to prove I am who I said I am yet?"

"Listen, sir, I need to know who—"

"Stop asking my name. Ring me back on this number once you get in touch with someone who actually matters. You have ten minutes."

He hung up.

And, as he waited, he watched the camera feed from

downstairs. The terrorists were well-armed. Each had an AK-47, with more bags of guns if they needed them. They were skinheads, all dressed the same, all lost children desperate for an identity.

He counted the hostages on the ground. Forty-two. Then he looked at Daniel, who was standing against the wall with his hands on his head.

What were they planning on doing to him?

The phone rang. Sullivan answered it quickly.

"Hello?

"This is Special Agent Larson. Who is it I'm speaking to?"

"I can't tell you that."

"Why not?"

"I just can't, and it's not important. I got away, and I am in the CCTV room right now, watching the terrorists downstairs. Do you want me to tell you what you're dealing with?"

"Okay, you have my attention."

"There are five terrorists. They are white supremacists. They have forty-two hostages, all in the downstairs reception area. They also have a black FBI agent who they've separated from the rest of the hostages called Daniel Winstead. They have killed... a lot of people."

"What's a lot?"

"They went through each room, eliminating anyone who stood in their way. The hostages they have downstairs are the only ones alive. If you enter, it will put all their lives at risk."

"You're not in the position to be telling us what to do, are you? For all I know, you could be one of them."Sullivan sighed. Just as he thought, he was dealing with idiots. "Sure. Believe what you want to believe. I've told you what the situation is, so my conscience is clear, and you can kindly fuck off."

Sullivan hung up. The ungrateful swine. The phone rang

again, but Sullivan rejected the call, silenced the phone, and chucked it on the floor.

He turned to the monitors. Searched for a way out. An escape route that would avoid the terrorists.

And he told himself that he had no reason to stay.

That he'd done more than most in his position would do to help.

That the voice at the back of his head was wrong. It was up to the FBI now.

Even though he'd sneaked through far more embassies, and killed far more villains, and fought far tougher opponents than any of the FBI agents outside, it didn't matter.

This was *not* his fight.

A monitor to the left displayed the corridor on the floor above. There was a door that led to the roof. That was Sullivan's escape route.

And it was time to take it.

He readied the gun, opened the door, and looked back and forth. The same silent destruction decorated the corridor. The same blood on formerly pristine walls. The same bodies slumped against doors.

He stepped out and ran to the stairwell, entered it, keeping his gun ready, then made it to the top floor. He entered the corridor and stopped, despairing at the amount of death.

If possible, there was even more bloodshed than on the previous floor. Even more carnage. Even more bodies.

Killing did not bother these people. They were ruthless. Happy to murder for their cause. Which meant that all of those hostages downstairs were in grave danger. Once the terrorists no longer saw them as collateral, or when the terrorists left—what then? They'd already shown that they did not value human life.

Sullivan was sure they would not risk leaving witnesses if they didn't need to.

"Fuck," Sullivan muttered, telling himself to stop ruminating about it.

It was not his problem.

He'd spoken to the FBI. He'd told them what they were dealing with. It was their problem now, and he had to trust they were competent. He had to believe they could handle it.

He strode through the corridor, stepping over limbs, ignoring the faces of wide-eyed corpses. He'd seen dead bodies before. It wasn't new.

But it didn't mean he should allow these terrorists to create any more dead bodies.

*Shut up. Just keep moving. You're almost there.*

He found the door to the roof. Took out the guard's keys. Found the key that fit, turned it, and walked up the steps.

From his place on the roof, he could see the FBI below. He could see nearby buildings. He could see incoming rain clouds. And he could see his freedom. He had several options of how to escape undetected.

He could jump to the next building.

Or he could climb down the fire escape.

Or he could jump, and land in the trash below—it would hurt, but it would cushion his fall. It was only three floors, after all, but he could make it—then he could be at the airport within an hour.

Or he could stay.

*Stop it.*

He could help save those hostages.

*No.*

He had been trained for this.

He knew how to fight better than anyone. He knew how to hunt better than anyone. And he knew how to handle a tense, life-or-death situation better than anyone.

At least, he used to. He'd just get in the way now.

He dropped his head and closed his eyes. That was an excuse.

And what of Daniel Winstead?

The man captured him. He was quite happy at the prospect of Sullivan on death row. Ecstatic, even.

This was Sullivan's opportunity to escape, to flee whilst attention was focussed on something else. This was his opportunity to get away and disappear into obscurity once again.

So why was he hesitating?

His stomach rumbled. He was sweating—part tiredness, part being an alcoholic—and he was getting incensed with that part of him that kept telling him to stay.

He needed to leave. Now. Get out of the country. Avoid capture. That's what Sullivan of old would have done. The Sullivan his government produced. The trained killer.

But Sullivan didn't want to be that man anymore, did he?

He hated that person. He loathed him. He lay awake at night, resenting him, thinking about how much he'd love to beat some sense into him.

The things that person had done, the questionable ethics he'd held, the ruthless decisions he made...

He felt bad about leaving now, and that was why he was different; why he was a changed man.

And that was exactly why he would not leave.

It was exactly why he was going to save Daniel Winstead and the hostages.

"For fuck's sake, Jay," he said to himself, shaking his head.

He bid goodbye to the adjacent buildings and the trash below and the fire escape he could climb down. He turned his back on them and went back inside.

This was the Jay Sullivan of new, and he could not let himself leave.

# CHAPTER TWENTY-FIVE

THE PHONE RANG.

Walter stared at it. Nervous. Excited.

He glanced at Curtis, who began bouncing, barely able to keep still.

"Well, go on!" Curtis urged. "Answer it!"

Walter took a deep breath, held it, and released it. This was it. Shit was about to happen.

Amateur hour was over, and all those other sects who thought Walter was full of inaction were about to watch in awe. He could just picture them, watching their televisions as the news broadcast an aerial shot of events, ruing how bad it made them look.

A wide grin spread between his cheeks.

He picked up the phone, placed it against his ear, and let the silence linger for a few seconds.

"What?" he grunted, intentionally elusive.

"Hello, this is Gary Cunningham." The man's voice was smooth and calm, like a late-night radio talk show host. "I'm with the FBI. Who am I talking to?"

"What the fuck is it to you?"

He caught sight of Curtis's smirk. This was better than any action movie they'd watched together.

"I just wish to know who it is I'm talking with," Gary continued.

"What, are you the FBI negotiator? You about to mind-fuck me, are you?"

"I am a negotiator, but that doesn't mean I'm going to mind-fuck you. I'm not here to tell you what to do. You're in charge, we both know that. I'm here to make sure this all runs smoothly. Is that okay with you?"

Walter was taken aback by the question.

He looked at Curtis, a little thrown but still gleeful. He turned to Herman, Simon and Corey, who gazed back at him, intrigued. His focus turned to Daniel, stood there, so contemptuous, keeping in all that petty little rage. Then he looked over at the hostages, each as terrified and pathetic as the last.

"Fine," Walter replied. "That's what I want, too."

"That's great. Now, what can I call you?"

"You can call me Walter."

"Walter, that's great, thank you. Now, tell me, Walter, who are you with?"

"With?"

"Are you part of a group?"

"We are the White Avengers."

"The White Avengers. I like it. It's strong—shows that you are really trying to stand up for our race."

Walter was confused. *Our* race? Why was this guy taking his side?

Maybe he was. Maybe their message was already getting through. Maybe they were lucky enough to speak to someone in the FBI who supported the cause and knew exactly how Walter felt.

Then it hit him. This guy wasn't taking his side.

This guy was trying to manipulate him.

Trying to make him think they were on the same team.

Fuck this guy.

"I know what you're doing," Walter said.

"What am I doing, Walter?"

"Fuck you. You don't give a shit about the white race. You sit with your fucking minorities and your immigrants and you fucking laugh at us, thinking *we're* the ones who are wrong, thinking *we* have the problem."

"I don't think you have a problem, Walter."

"Oh yeah? You agree with me then?"

"If I'm honest, it's not something I've considered. Why don't you tell me what it is you don't like about minorities and immigrants?"

It was a shock to hear an FBI agent repeat back those words. It didn't sound right. Like something that tasted delicious to him, and that this man only pretended to like.

"You have no idea," Walter said, his voice a low grumble.

"Then please tell me."

"You don't care."

"I wouldn't be asking if I didn't care, Walter."

"Then why aren't you with us? Why aren't you in here, standing up for the white race?"

"Because I haven't heard your point of view before. But I want to hear it now. Why don't you tell me what you dislike about these people?"

Walter looked at Daniel. Glared at him. At the expensive suit he didn't deserve. At the way he stood proudly despite being their hostage. At the way he'd taken a job a white man could have had.

"Everything," Walter growled.

"Such as?"

"Such as everything. How they take our jobs. Take our women. Rape our people."

Walter had never met an immigrant who took their jobs, or their women, or raped anyone. But they were words he was used to saying; like a human pamphlet, ready to repeat his propaganda.

"That must be frustrating," Gary said.

"You have no idea. And we are the only ones who see it."

"Oh, I see it, Walter, really I do."

"No, you don't."

"Every day when I walk down the street, I see them, in their groups. I feel intimidated by them. Do you ever feel intimidated, Walter?"

"No." Walter would die before he admitted to being intimidated by those people.

"Then I'm glad that there are people like you who will protect me, Walter."

"Why do you keep saying my name like that?"

"Like what?"

"Like you're saying it on purpose. Is this some negotiating technique or something—do you keep saying my name to, like, make me like you or some shit?"

"Not at all. I'm just trying to understand."

"I don't give a fuck if you understand."

"That's a shame, because I'd like to."

Walter paced to the end of the hallway and back, clutching his gun. The power to take a life rested beneath his fingers, and it was a power that so few people ever experienced.

He had that power, and he wouldn't let these people forget that.

"Cut the shit," Walter decided. "You don't care about getting to know me any more than I care about getting to know you."

"Then what would you like to talk about?"

"I want to get down to business."

"Yes?"

"I want to stop dancing around, talking about shit you don't care about." He gesticulated with his gun as he talked. "I want to get into what we want."

"What do you want, Walter?"

Walter stopped pacing and grinned. "Now, that is the right question."

# CHAPTER TWENTY-SIX

WHEN GARY CUNNINGHAM HAD WOKEN UP THAT morning, he'd looked forward to taking his child to school. His wife had left a coffee and a banana on his bedside table for him when she'd left for her shift at the hospital. The sun was shining, and it had the makings of a glorious day.

As his daughter sang along to *SpongeBob SquarePants,* he poured her fresh orange juice and buttered her toast. She ate it, then dressed herself, then flung her arms around him and told him he was the best daddy she'd ever had.

He was going to point out that he was the only daddy she'd ever had, but didn't. Instead, he told her she was the best daughter he'd ever had, and enjoyed hearing her laugh. He wished he could capture that laugh and take it with him everywhere. Then, they made sure all her schoolbooks were in her bags. He'd put her in the car seat in the back of his people carrier, and driven to school with the CD of nursery rhymes playing.

He'd been halfway home when he realised he was still listening to *Humpty Dumpty*.

That's when he'd made the mistake of putting the radio

on. The news reporter's voice sounded louder than usual, and his announcement of an emerging hostage situation at The British Embassy filled the car in surround sound.

This was Gary's day off.

It was his day to relax.

He had plans. Grand plans. He was going to play golf, then pick his daughter up from school and take her to the playground, going past the sweet shop on the way home to let her pick whichever sweets she'd like.

When his wife called a few minutes later, her voice replaced the radio through the speakers of the car, and she asked if he'd heard the news.

"Yeah, I heard it all right," he admitted. He didn't hide the resentment in his voice.

"It's okay. I'll be able to pick Stacey up from school."

"We don't know yet if—"

"Gary, we both know. I'll pick her up from school. You go help people."

Gary sighed. He wanted to protest, but it wouldn't do any good. He was fortunate, he guessed, that his wife was such a patient, understanding woman.

"Thank you," he said.

"I love you."

"I love you too."

Less than two minutes later, Gary was pulling up in his driveway as the dreaded phone call lit up his phone. He saw his boss's name. He knew what this was. And he knew he didn't have any choice but to answer it.

"Yep, I've heard it," he said as he answered the phone.

"We need you."

"I'll be there in ten minutes."

He didn't even bother going back inside the house. He set off, mentally preparing as quickly as he could.

You don't become one of the FBI's best chief negotiators

based in New York, and not expect to have to respond to a hostage situation as it emerges down the road.

Truth is, he spent most of his days training students in the academy, teaching them techniques they'd probably forget as soon as they were in the field. He often wondered how well these young men and women put his lessons into practice once the job put them into a high-pressured situation, with the adrenaline running and your words becoming jumbled in your mind.

And so that was how he ended up here, outside The British Embassy, with a phone attached to his ear, speaking to a notorious racist—Walter Franks—and pretending to sympathise with his ridiculous ideology.

The most important part of any negotiation is 'active listening.' You don't listen to judge, but to understand. You mirror their words and phrases, and sympathise with their plight. This is especially difficult when they claim black people "rape our women". What he'd ideally like to say is, "Where exactly are you getting your information from?" then follow this up with "and please, tell me your exact statistics that show this, as I think you are talking utter nonsense?"

But one cannot.

So instead, he answered, "That must be frustrating," as if this idiot's opinion was valid, and not an embarrassment to a nation he'd spent so many years defending.

After active listening and empathy comes 'rapport.' It's not that you agree with their ideology, but that you don't disagree. You adopt the ideology to an extent—enough to make them feel like they know you well enough that, once this is all over, you'll go for a beer with them. Hell, make them think they can date your sister if you need to, or join you at a ball game, or give you a big bear hug as he leaves the building—whatever it takes to make them trust you. Truth was, he wanted to see the guy put in cuffs and left to rot in prison.

"I want to stop dancing around, talking about shit you don't care about. I want to get into what we want."

Gary twirled a pen in his hand. His hands always fidgeted during negotiations, and he usually needed something to fiddle with.

"What do you want, Walter?" he asked, hoping the frown on his face did not come across in the tone of his voice.

"Now that is the right question," Walter replied. This guy seemed to think he was Bruce Willis, or Jason Statham, or some other badass action guy. But he wasn't. He wasn't even worthy of being called a movie villain—he was the ant the villain stepped on. The dung on the bad guy's feet. The shit the hero's nemesis flushed down the toilet.

Gary looked at his boss as Walter listed his demands—the removal of immigrants in both the UK and the US, the reintroduction of segregation, the restoration of Donald Trump to power—and, as Gary held his boss's gaze, he shook his head, knowing the FBI couldn't give in to any of these demands. Not only were they ethically wrong, they were ridiculous and farfetched. At least professional criminals came up with realistic demands, such as the release of a hostage—the idea that the FBI could follow through on any of Walter's instructions just showed how deluded the guy was. There was a vast distance between this guy's version of reality and the world everyone else lived in.

It became apparent to Gary that there wasn't much he could do with this guy, and that negotiations would likely fail.

# CHAPTER TWENTY-SEVEN

THE FIRST THING SULLIVAN NEEDED WAS A BETTER WEAPON.

He hated guns.

He'd once been known as 'the assassin without a gun'—he hadn't needed one; his environment was his weapon. A stapler, a doorknob, or even a pen were all items he could make deadly. As such, he had never spent much time developing his skills with guns. Besides, they were heavy and clunky things; a true fighter should be able to use better weapons.

This was something Sullivan slightly regretted now. He wasn't as nimble and adept as he once was, and being able to take out a target from afar would be useful.

But if he was going to do anything to make a difference here, he needed to tap into his skill set. Be the Sullivan of now in his mind, but the Sullivan of old in his ruthlessness.

"What the fuck are you on about..." Sullivan murmured to himself, suddenly aware of the rambling, nonsensical nature of his thoughts. He crept down the steps from the roof, placing little pressure on each foot to avoid making noise.

Not that there was anyone up here. As far as the terrorists

were concerned, everyone up here was dead. He could roam about unnoticed, so long as he did nothing stupid to give himself away.

But roaming about here unnoticed would do nothing to defeat the terrorists, would it? Eventually, he would have to make his presence known. He just had to play it the right way —whatever that way was.

And so he returned to his dilemma: the need to find a weapon.

He needed a kitchen. Or a staff room with an area for making food. That was where he'd most likely find a knife.

He stepped over the bodies—which were now as part of the décor as the paint and the plants—and edged past each room. A few doors down, he found an open door to a kitchen and a lady's body slumped over the table, her head beside a half-eaten plate of toast.

He entered, scanning the room, and made his way to the cutlery drawer. He found a set of sharp knives inside. He took the biggest one and placed it down the back of his trousers.

Then he turned to leave. And stopped. Noticed something.

A framed picture on the wall.

A man in a police officer's uniform, shaking hands with a man in a suit with a smarmy politician's smile.

Sullivan assumed it was of someone who meant something. Someone who mattered to everyone else. Perhaps it was meant as a source of inspiration to his subordinates, but for whoever had accepted that award, it portrayed nothing more than arrogance.

Then again, maybe that was just Sullivan's bias, as he remembered there being a similar photograph in his child-hood home.

It was above the dining table. The one they rarely used. They had a dining table to pretend to guests that they gathered around it and shared stories of their day. It was a table that made people think that this was a normal family. In truth, they ate on their laps in front of the television, often watching the news so Dad could rant about whatever person was doing what to whom.

But that picture...

Sullivan often walked in on Dad staring at it. Sometimes with his hands in his pockets, sometimes by his side, but usually accompanied by an affirmative nod, or glint in his eye, or a swelling of pride.

"Come here, boy," Dad had once said, and Sullivan had readied himself for a punch. Only this time, Dad had put his arm around his son. "See this? This is the mayor. And that's me, getting an award. Your dad's a hero. How does that feel?"

*How does that feel?*

At the time, he said the right thing. Used words like proud, patriotic, and amazed. It made Sullivan the child feel nothing, and in retrospect, it made Sullivan the adult feel sick. It highlighted how someone can seem like the perfect man to the rest of society, but a real bastard behind closed doors. It showed that people gave awards to those who present themselves as heroes, whilst actual heroes suffer through their pain without ever being recognised.

"Maybe someday you'll join the force, and you can have a medal just like your dad."

Dad's arm had felt strange around Sullivan. Like a venomous snake that cuddled him instead of wrapping its body around his neck and asphyxiating him. It felt like a trap, somehow.

Then his dad snorted away a laugh. "Or maybe not. Who knows, stranger things have happened. Kids like you normally end up picking up my garbage, not locking away criminals."

And Dad's hand, just as easily as it had arrived around Sullivan's shoulders, slithered away and entered his pockets.

A few years later, Sullivan learned his dad had received the award for putting away a criminal they'd been after for a while. A black man named Troy Evans. A man who, a few years after Dad's death, was exonerated following the use of DNA evidence to prove his innocence. He was paid thousands of pounds in damages for the time he'd had to serve. It still didn't make the news, though, and the world saw his father's murder-suicide as a tragedy, rather than the self-destruction of a racist cop.

"You really were a prick, weren't you?" Sullivan found himself saying. An attack of emotions surprised him; feelings that hadn't surfaced for many years.

Ones that he quelled, reminding himself that he needed to focus.

He left the room, crept along the corridor, and down the stairs to the ground floor.

He opened the door to the corridor, just a few inches, and could hear a voice from the other end where the passageway opened out into the reception area. He couldn't hear the response to this voice, and assumed they were on the phone. Perhaps with the FBI negotiator.

Step one in 'How to Deal with a Terrorist Hostage Situation'. Classic. And useless. But the best option, all things considered.

But it wouldn't work.

These terrorists didn't care about their hostages. They had an endgame in mind and, as amateurish as they were, their madness was ensuring their dominance, and they were winning.

Sullivan kept himself against the wall of the corridor, tiptoeing silently toward the foyer where the hostages were contained, and listened.

# CHAPTER TWENTY-EIGHT

CURTIS DID NOT LISTEN TO WHAT WAS GOING ON AROUND him. Someone would start talking about this or that, and his mind would start thinking about the colours of the room, or what people were doing at the next table, or repeating a jingle from an advert he'd recently heard. It was a problem he'd always had.

Although he would use the word *problem* loosely.

Teachers found it a problem. Parents found it a problem. The doctors who slapped an ADHD diagnosis on him found it a problem.

Curtis had never had a *problem* with it.

Perhaps people should try harder to keep his attention. It wasn't his fault that what they had to say wasn't interesting.

And, as Walter ranted at the negotiator, Curtis's mind couldn't help but wander once more.

"–and I'm fed up of Islamic laws being forced on a Christian nation; I'm fed up with the leaders who allow a dilution of a beautiful, pure race; I'm fed up with superior genetics being diluted and fucked around with—"

Curtis's eyes scanned the room, surveying the marble

pillars holding up the grand ceiling, the tiled black-and-white floor, the posh tables, the reception desk beside a padded leather chair; all the rich shit that doesn't need to be here.

"—we brought them over here as slaves, not as equals, and your fucking human rights shit has meant they think they are better than us, and none of the politicians seem to realise that we are striving to save the white race here, *their* race—"

He noticed the chandelier above him. A chandelier... What the hell is a chandelier doing in The British Embassy? If you lose your passport, you hardly need a chandelier to make you feel better, do you?

"—there is a race war coming, Manson saw it all those years ago, so has every other person with their head screwed on, so why can't the politicians see it, hey? And when this war gets here, whose side are they going to be on? Because peace has no side, I'll tell you that—"

Curtis's eyes wandered from the chandelier to the pillar to the floor to the hostages. On their knees with their heads on the tiles, just as they had been instructed. Their legs must ache by now. How long had they been like that?

Curtis scoffed.

No one would ever make him get on his knees.

If someone put a gun to his face and told him to kneel, he would tell them to eat shit. They'd have to shoot him. There was not a chance he would bow down to anyone.

He focused on a few of the hostages more closely. A tall, gangly man in a suit covered his head. He was shaking. Curtis snorted. What a coward. Did this man have no pride?

Beside him, a smaller Latino man in janitor's overalls kept his eyes closed as his forehead rested against the hard surface of the floor.

Beside him was a woman.

Now this woman was a tasty bit of something!

Slightly podgy, but Curtis never minded that; as his father

always used to say, "It gives me something to hold on to." She wore a knee-length dress with black tights. A neat, brown cardigan. Brunette hair pulled back into a ponytail. Maybe late thirties, early forties. She had a sizeable backside, and it was on full display since she was on her knees. It was a backside he'd love to pound. He could just imagine it rippling as he thrust inside of her.

"Hey," Curtis whispered.

A few hostages flinched.

"Hey, I'm talking to you."

A few turned their heads cautiously to the side.

"Woman, I mean you."

The woman in question turned her head further.

"Yes, that's it. Stand up."

She looked around, searching for who else he could be talking to.

"*You*, bitch."

She rose slowly, her knees buckling, hugging her body, her mascara smudged. She looked both appetising and pathetic.

"Come over here."

She looked around, as if someone was going to help her. No one did. She stepped over the crouched bodies, her high heels making a gentle echo, careful not to step on anyone.

"That's it, a little closer."

The woman stepped over another hostage and paused a few steps away from Curtis. Her entire body was shaking. Terror dripped down her face. It was highly arousing.

"Closer," he said, enjoying her fear. She wore too much makeup. She probably wasn't the thin, attractive woman she was in her twenties, but she didn't need to try so hard to compensate for that. Age brings beauty, and it saddened Curtis that she didn't realise that.

"Closer," he repeated.

She stepped forward.

"A little closer," he repeated.

She stepped forward again.

"If you don't get yourself here, now, I am going to gut you."

She began crying and tried to stifle it. She shuffled toward Curtis until she reached the edge of his personal space, her arms still wrapped around her torso, her knees shaking. Her terror made Curtis hard.

Her name badge read *Wendy*.

"Wendy. That your name?"

She nodded.

"It's a lovely name. Do you like it?"

She paused, then shrugged; a slight movement that Curtis could barely see.

"I'm going to be your Peter Pan, Wendy. How does that sound?"

She closed her eyes, bowed her head, and cried some more.

"Get on your knees."

She hesitated.

"Now."

Slowly, she lowered herself to her knees.

Curtis stood, so his crotch was within inches of her face. He hadn't showered in days and he stank of piss. He didn't care. He liked the idea of her revulsion as his rancid aromas drifted toward her. He wanted her to hate every minute of this. He relished watching her squirm.

"We have a bit of time to kill, Wendy," Curtis said, glancing at Daniel, who glared back at him.

Curtis held his gun up high so Daniel would know not to try anything.

"Let's have some fun."

# CHAPTER TWENTY-NINE

SULLIVAN WATCHED WALTER FROM AROUND THE CORNER OF the corridor as he continued his ridiculous diatribe down the phone, ranting about immigrants and genetics and race, and all that other crap fools like him believe.

At first, he'd believed that Walter was in charge; and hell, Walter probably believed he was too. Yet, as he watched, it slowly dawned on Sullivan that Walter wasn't the biggest threat.

It was the topless man with the blacked-out eyes.

Sullivan vaguely recognised him. A memory, slightly out of focus, of his knuckles coming toward him. Perhaps Sullivan had met the man whilst drunk. Had a fight with him.

Probably—he seemed the kind of fool Sullivan would pick a fight with.

But whilst Walter was clearly the one in charge, Curtis was the one who held the most authority. His appearance was inhuman, his walk was predatory, and his stance was animalistic. He strutted around like a lion watching over its territory. He had levels of arrogance and insanity that made someone dangerous; when someone's that unhinged, even they don't know what they might do next.

And he was beckoning a hostage closer. A woman, who he had forced to her knees.

Sullivan's fingers flexed around his knife. His body tensed. He hated this monster, but he had to be cool. Revealing himself now wasn't the answer. He had to find a better way to take the terrorists out. Lure them away, somehow, and do it one by one. Yet the more Curtis did to this woman, the harder he struggled not to act. And, as Curtis placed the tip of his AK-47 against her nose, it grew even tougher to contain himself. She whimpered, and he told her to cry silently. Then he told her to open her mouth.

He instructed her to suck the end of the gun.

Sullivan almost threw himself out from his hiding place, but held himself back. He could see Daniel thinking the same thing, watching Curtis, wishing he had a way to stop him.

What if Sullivan ran?

What if he ran hard toward Curtis, and stuck the knife in his throat?

But then what?

If Curtis could fight, then Sullivan might not kill him instantly, and they may end up in combat. Which meant the other four could shoot him. Or, worse, they might kill a hostage.

No, Sullivan had to remove his emotions. Detach himself from what he was seeing.

But, with tears trickling down the woman's cheeks as she moved her head back and forth, running her lips up and down the shaft of the gun, he found it difficult.

Then he saw Curtis's face, and he found it almost impossible.

It was a look of demented pleasure; of twisted arousal; of complete and utter delight. Curtis was gaining all kinds of gratification from this woman's degradation—the humiliation of sucking a gun was living out a fantasy Curtis had probably harboured for a long time.

Sullivan glanced at Walter. Oblivious to what Curtis was doing. Too busy ranting down the phone.

"—and it's the Hispanics that need to fuck off back to where they came from, Mexico or whatever, and they need to stay in their own fucking country and not bring their problems over here—"

Sullivan closed his eyes. Told himself this was stupid. Told himself this was not a good plan.

Then, unable to stop himself from intervening, he did it anyway.

"Oi, you little prick!" he bellowed at Curtis, who swiped the gun out of the woman's mouth, shoving her to the floor, and aimed the gun at the direction of Sullivan's voice.

"Show yourself!" Curtis demanded.

"What the fuck is wrong with you?" Sullivan demanded.

Curtis shot at Sullivan. A stream of bullets hit the wall opposite Sullivan, narrowly missing him as he turned back down the corridor.

"You've done it now," he told himself as he sprinted back toward the stairwell.

---

Curtis emptied his ammunition at the corner of the corridor, then reloaded, striding toward the sound of the voice.

"What the fuck?" Walter shouted. "I thought you dealt with everyone?"

"I did!" Curtis barked.

"Walter, Walter, are you there?" came a small voice from the phone receiver. "Walter, talk to me. I hear gunshots, what's happening?"

"Fucking get them!" Walter demanded, the negotiator no longer his priority. "Go, now!"

"Walter? What's going on?"

Walter slammed down the phone.

It started ringing again almost instantly, but no one answered.

Curtis ran into the corridor and saw a man disappear up the stairwell. He shot at the direction of the silhouette, but it disappeared up the stairs.

He sprinted down the corridor, followed by Simon and Corey. They ran, but not as fast as Curtis—no one was as eager for blood, and no one was more annoyed at missing the opportunity for the kill.

He barged open the door to the stairwell with his shoulder and didn't hesitate before shooting upwards.

But the door to the next floor was already closing.

He ran up the stairs, his comrades trailing behind, determined to shed this bastard's blood.

———

"Well done, Jay, really well done."

He ran across the first-floor corridor, hearing the bullets ricochet off the other side of the door to the stairwell.

"You've really ballsed it up this time, you idiot."

He looked through the window of one room, then another. He needed somewhere to hide. To wait. Somewhere with plenty of cover. His strategy had to be patience; he would wait for the right moment, when he had them isolated, and take them out one by one.

He chose a room, entered it, and shut the door quietly behind him.

# CHAPTER THIRTY

THE PHONE, HELD STIFFLY AT GARY'S EAR, KEPT RINGING, and ringing, and ringing, and ringing.

Most of them thought they might have heard gunshots from within the building—but Gary knew he'd heard them down the phone. They were far louder through a speaker he held to his ear than they were from deep inside a building. He was desperate to talk to Walter and find out what was going on.

But the phone just kept ringing.

Eventually, Gary dropped the phone to his side and turned to his boss.

"He's not answering."

"Then try again."

"He's not—"

"This is our only avenue, dammit. Try again!"

He was right.

Gary was their best, if not their only, hope.

They couldn't enter. Not with that many hostages. They couldn't risk that many lives.

They had snipers on the roofs, but they couldn't risk a

shot through the window. They couldn't take the chance of hitting a civilian.

Without lethal force or ability to gain entry, all they had were negotiations.

Gary tried again. Put the phone to his ear. Let it ring. It slid around his sweaty palm. His fingers were furiously kneading his tie.

"Come on... come on..."

There were so many eyes looking in his direction.

Everyone was expectant.

And Walter was not answering the phone.

"Come on!"

He kicked the nearby car. Began pacing. He felt agitated. Number one rule was you stay calm. He'd taught his students that. And he tried to remind himself of that.

But he'd heard gunshots. He'd heard a confrontation. Behind Walter's nonsensical ranting, he'd heard more of them, and they were arguing.

He huffed. Tried to ignore everyone's stares. Tried to imagine he was on his own, at home, a phone against his ear, ringing to reserve a table at a restaurant.

It was a technique he taught his students: picture yourself somewhere calm, and forget, just for a moment, where you are and what you are doing.

But the phone just kept ringing.

He turned to his boss. Shook his head.

"Keep trying," his boss instructed.

"I can keep trying, but—"

"We have at least forty hostages in there. We have FBI agents in there. We have civilians. Please, Gary, just—"

"What do you want me to do?" Gary snapped. "I can't force him to talk to me if he doesn't even pick up the damn phone, can I?"

His boss placed a calming hand on his shoulder.

"I know, Gary. But this is our best option. Please, just keep trying."

Gary nodded. Focused on his breathing. Kept it calm. He'd dealt with these types of people plenty of times.

He kept ringing.

But Walter never answered.

# CHAPTER THIRTY-ONE

SIMON CLUTCHED HIS GUN IN BOTH HANDS, TRAILING behind Corey and Curtis. He hadn't wanted to kill anyone; that wasn't why he did this. He wanted to stand up for his race, not see people die. Especially white people, who made up most of today's death toll.

But Curtis was unhinged.

Walter might be in charge, but that was only because it suited Curtis at this moment. Once Curtis decided more blood needed to be shed than Walter was comfortable with, the balance would change.

And would Simon stand up to Curtis?

Hell, no.

Simon was just a simple boy from Texas. He wasn't John Wayne; he was the guy who backed John Wayne up. He wasn't brave. He wasn't a leader. He was a lemming who would do whatever he must to survive. He was a misfit, searching for identity, craving revenge on the bullies who stole his lunch money when he was a child. It was such a high school cliché, and he resented how stereotypical it was—the unpopular kid being pushed around by the jocks. But that was who he was.

And now look at him.

Those jocks would be scared.

This may not have been what he wanted, or how he wanted to do it—but this was how it was now, and he didn't have a clue.

He came to a halt behind Curtis as they entered the corridor. Each room was quiet. The corpses they'd created remained undisturbed.

They listened and waited.

There was no sound.

"He has to be in one of these rooms," Curtis whispered. "He didn't have time to get to the end of the corridor."

Curtis peered through a window.

"We each take a room," he said. "Then go onto another. We do this quickly."

"Should we not stay together?"

Curtis frowned at him. "Why?"

"What if he's got a gun?"

"He's a loose hostage. He's a nobody. He won't be hard to take down—you see him, you shoot him. You got a problem with that?"

Yes, he had a problem with that.

Simon had a huge problem with that.

But would he dare say that to Curtis?

Would he hell.

"Okay," he confirmed, and Curtis moved slowly and silently to the first room, pushing the door ajar, and moving in. Corey did the same with the next. Simon took a deep breath and entered the next room along.

It was a small office. Two desks, quite close together. Name plates on the desks for people who were either downstairs, or dead.

He stepped over a body, flinching at the sight. Why did these corpses all have their eyes open? They were like those creepy paintings where the eyes follow you around the room. Wherever he stepped, that dead body watched him, reminding him of what he had done.

He had just wanted to stand up for his race, but this was really fucked up.

He edged into the room, peered under the first desk, then under the other, and backed out again.

Curtis and Corey were already in the next few rooms along, so Simon passed them and entered another office.

This time, there was only one desk. A beefy man with big arms sat in a leather seat, his head slumped on his shoulder, a bullet hole oozing blood from his forehead.

Simon gagged. Looked under the desk. Scanned the room again. Left.

The next room was a men's bathroom. He entered, greeted by four urinals and the smell of shit.

He crept forward. Four cubicles. Each door was closed, but not locked.

He nudged the first open with his foot. The door swung slowly to the side. A man sat on the toilet with his trousers around his ankles and bullet holes in his chest. What a way to go. The door swung back again and closed.

He moved to the second. Nudged the door open. Empty.

Then there came a slight scuffle. From the next cubicle. The shadows beneath the door flickered.

Was this him?

He pointed his gun at the door, his finger on the trigger, ready to squeeze as soon as he saw a face.

He nudged the door open with his foot.

It revealed nothing.

He must have been hearing things. He was on high alert;

the adrenaline was running—his mind could be playing tricks on him.

Man, how he hated this.

He reached the last door and kicked it open to reveal another empty cubicle.

He let out a breath and dropped the gun to his side. His body relaxed, and he began his walk to the exit, but just as he passed the second cubicle, something burst out of it, grabbed his head, and pounded it onto the sink.

The stranger twisted the gun out of Simon's hand and kicked it across the room. He covered Simon's mouth from behind so he couldn't scream, then lifted his head so he could see himself and the pale face of his assailant in the mirror.

How had the guy done that?

The space beneath the cubicle... He must have sneaked beneath cubicle walls, moving to the first cubicle as Simon moved to the second.

The man placed his arm around Simon's neck and choked him, covering his mouth so Simon couldn't make any noise. Simon placed his feet on the sink and pushed, forcing them backwards, through the door of the cubicle. The man sat on the toilet and squeezed harder and harder on Simon's neck.

Simon tried to talk, tried to reason with the man, to say he didn't want to do this – but the man would not take his hand from Simon's mouth.

Simon struggled as much as he could, kicking his body, thrashing his arms, elbowing his legs, twisting his torso.

The man held on.

Somehow, he held on.

It was only now, as the world lost focus, that he realised he was about to die. Funny, the thought hadn't come to him yet. He'd been determined to fight, sure that he could beat this man, positive he could defeat some ordinary civilian.

But this wasn't an ordinary civilian.

This was a man who knew how to kill.

And, as he felt his consciousness fade, he felt afraid—gravely afraid—then he was gone, and his body was devoid of life.

# CHAPTER THIRTY-TWO

WHEN A MAN IS BEING ASPHYXIATED, HE USUALLY FALLS unconscious before he dies.

This was why Sullivan held onto this man's throat long after the body went limp. Once he was sure the man would not get up, he left him on the toilet—adding another body to the many others these terrorists had created.

When the men had entered the floor, hunting Sullivan, he'd peered out from his hiding place and counted three of them. Now there were two. If he could dispose of the next two, then he'd only have two downstairs left to deal with.

He took a deep breath.

Why did this shit keep happening to him?

He just wanted a quiet place to drink away his days. Somewhere he could fade out of existence, barely a memory to anyone who walked past him. Instead, the FBI just had to interfere with him, and now here he was. The life he tried to leave had found him again.

He didn't want to kill people.

He really didn't.

Yet, somehow, this life kept finding its way back to him.

He stepped out of the cubicle and avoided his reflection above the sinks. He paused by the exit, listening to see if anyone was walking past.

He placed his hand on the door and nudged it open, ever so slightly, so he was just able to peer out.

Further along the corridor, the other two men went into separate rooms.

Sullivan stepped into the corridor, and let the door close silently behind him. He crept, ensuring not to make a sound, until he reached another office.

Through the door, he saw his second target.

————

Corey looked under the table. Under another desk. In the cupboard.

It was another empty room.

Where the hell was this man?

He turned back to the door, sure they wouldn't find him, only for the door to slam against his nose.

He stumbled back into the room, and the stranger entered, swiping his feet out from beneath him and sending him flying to his back.

He pulled the trigger as he fell, trying to aim it at the stranger, but instead shot pieces of plaster out of the ceiling.

He tried to recover, but the stranger landed a knee into his chest, winding him. He lifted his weapon, but the man pinned his gun arm down.

The stranger lifted a knife high above his head, and it glistened in the reflection of the sun outside of the window in the brief second before it soared through the air and entered his neck, creating a long, clean slit across the length of his throat

He was sure that Curtis would have heard the gunshots.

But it was too late for Corey.

He was clutching his neck, blood seeping through his fingers, feeling nothing but agony, tortured by the thought of imminent death, and staring at the stranger.

The stranger took Corey's gun, abruptly stood, and aimed it at the doorway. As Corey's fingers scrambled over the open wound of his neck—like he could do anything to stop the bleeding—he saw Curtis in the doorway, pointing his gun back at his killer.

Then the pain became too much—as did the thought that his kid would grow up without a dad; a thought that echoed over and over in his mind.

And, as the blood squirted from his throat and onto the trousers of the stranger, the pain subsided into numbness, the world faded to black and, in his final thought, he decided that he'd lived his life all wrong.

———

"I know you."

True, Sullivan recognised this man too—after all, the bloke's appearance was quite distinctive—but he didn't feel like talking.

Yet talking may be all he had.

It was a good, old-fashioned stand-off. Each of them pointing a gun at the other. Metres apart. Knowing a slight movement on either side would probably result in both their deaths.

This was about manipulation. The psychological advantage. Knowing that whoever kept the power would outdo the other.

"I knocked you out the other night, didn't I?" Curtis continued.

Was that how Sullivan knew him? Had the guy beat him in a fight?

"Yeah, you were pissed, and I beat the shit out of you," Curtis said, beaming at the memory. "It was glorious."

It all became clear. The faded memory, the glimpses of blurred movement—he'd had a drunken brawl. And he'd lost.

Sullivan *hated* losing.

"But I know your face, don't I? You were on that show... the most wanted... what was your name..." Curtis's face lit up. "Holy fuck, you're Jay Sullivan! An assassin. Holy shit, I'm about to kill an assassin. I can't believe it."

Sullivan almost said, *you are not about to kill me*, but didn't. He remained silent. Let this guy do the talking. He seemed to like it.

"Jesus, man, you're like a legend, aren't you? It's a shame you're not with us. You'd be great for our cause."

Sullivan snorted back a laugh. He couldn't help it.

"You think you're better than us, don't you?" Curtis said. "Think you got the bigger balls?"

"Yeah. Without a doubt."

Dammit. He'd been sucked in.

"See, it's fools like you that mean the white man will never get back what he deserves."

"And what exactly does he deserve?"

"Power."

"The white man already has the power. Have you not looked at the people who rule your country lately? Almost every one of them – white."

"The only time I look at politicians is when I'm stepping over their body. Now drop the gun."

Curtis tightened the grip on his gun. Sullivan held his steady. He hated how it felt in his hand, but it was the only thing standing between him and death, so he was going to hold on to it.

"Drop it," Curtis said. "And I promise to make it quick."

"You think this is the first time I've ever had a gun in my face?"

Curtis grinned. "Oh, you are tiresome," he said.

"Me, tiresome? Have you met you?"

Curtis sighed. "Tell you what..." He backed up. Sullivan frowned, unsure what Curtis was doing. Then Curtis stepped out of the room, so they were pointing guns at each other from either side of the open door.

"I think I can make you drop your gun..."

Curtis pulled the door closed and shoved his gun through the handle to block Sullivan's escape. Sullivan ran to the door and watched Curtis through the small window.

Curtis took another gun from his belt, licked his lips, and ran back across the corridor.

Sullivan tried opening the door. It wouldn't budge. He stepped back and ran at the door, barging it with his shoulder. It buckled, but did not open.

He stepped back and charged again. It hurt his shoulder more than it hurt the door.

With a longer run up, and a snarl across his face, he ran hard against the door, and finally barged it open.

He turned to the corridor, gun still in his hand, and sprinted, leaping across the bodies. He entered the stairwell and descended two steps at a time. Entered the next corridor. Ran through it, keeping his gun raised, skidded to a halt just before he reached the opening to the reception area, and used the corridor as cover.

"Oh, Mr Sullivan!" Curtis sang out.

Sullivan peered around the corridor. Curtis had his gun to the head of the woman he was tormenting earlier.

"Be a doll and throw me your gun, would you?"

Fine. Sullivan didn't want the gun anyway. He threw it out from behind the corridor, toward Curtis.

"Lovely. Now why don't you come out here and join us?"

Sullivan's body tensed. His mind raced through the options. Step out, and be killed. Don't step out and let the hostage be killed. Step out, be killed, and the hostage will be killed anyway.

He punched the wall.

Why was it always him?

"Step out, *now*."

"No!" Sullivan shouted.

"Step out, or I will kill this hostage, then I will kill another for every minute you delay."

Sullivan ran his hands through his hair. Stepped back and forth. Contemplated how much he hated himself and his sorry, pathetic life. Wondered what his father would say if he could see him now.

He saw much of his father in these racist lemmings. It made him hate them more.

"Do it now, Sullivan, or I will shoot this woman, and it will be your fault."

# CHAPTER THIRTY-THREE

DANIEL LOOKED FROM THE HOSTAGE, TO CURTIS, TO Walter. From the distraught face of the woman on her knees, to the psychotic pleasure of the nutcase, to the confused leadership of the man who stood beside an incessantly ringing phone.

"Did you say Jay Sullivan?" Walter asked.

"Yep," Curtis confirmed, keeping one hand on the woman's collar and the other on the gun pressed against her temple. "And he killed Simon and Corey."

"He did *what?*"

Daniel dropped his head. Oh, you fool. Sullivan had killed two of them.

He probably thought he was helping, but all he'd done was sign the death warrant of a few more hostages.

Sullivan had a tough choice to make—either be selfless and give himself up; or let more people die. And Daniel didn't have that much faith in Sullivan being selfless.

They needed to leave it to the negotiator. That was their best chance.

Then again, even the best chance was a small chance.

Daniel had already run through the possibilities of what they planned to do with him. They clearly wanted a black man to create some kind of a public statement—and him being an FBI agent was a bonus. Whatever happened, he wouldn't cooperate.

Then again, if he was uncooperative, he'd just wind them up, and would then be no different to Sullivan.

"Let the woman go!" Sullivan called out.

"I'm losing my patience, Sullivan," Curtis said.

Curtis was becoming more unhinged by the second. He was furious; Sullivan tended to have that effect on people. He'd just killed two of Curtis's friends, and this man wanted blood. The chaotic changes in the pitch of Curtis's voice only served as a reminder that his mind didn't function like everyone else's.

"You're just going to kill her anyway."

"You want to take that risk?"

"Let her go, then I'll come out."

"You have ten seconds, Sullivan."

Daniel bowed his head. Part of him didn't want to look; the other part knew that he needed to be a witness to what was happening. What if he needed to testify?

He almost cried.

Testify?

How about survival first, you idiot. Once he'd endured this ordeal, then he could consider the repercussions for these deluded terrorists.

"Ten."

Jesus, Sullivan, what are you doing?

If you're going to make a move—if you have something planned—do it now, for Christ's sake.

"Nine."

The woman bawled. She didn't care for dignity or

restraint. She cared for the child she had at home. She cared for a life that should have many years left in it.

Daniel was friends with Wendy. She used to work with him at the FBI, and would always have a smile ready for him when he walked into the office. She shared her cakes with him. Once, when he'd been stressed from the pressure the job put on his marriage, she'd brought him a coffee to cheer him up. She was so thoughtful.

She was a strong, kind woman.

And now she was on her knees, crying for her life.

"Eight."

Fuck, Sullivan.

Come on.

Stop this.

She doesn't deserve to die.

"Seven."

Daniel glared at their captors.

Three terrorists left.

Walter was engrossed in Curtis's countdown. No idea what his comrade was going to do. Just like the rest of them, he was unsure whether Wendy would be alive in a minute's time.

"Six."

She deserves life! She is entitled to it!

Why is this happening?

Because they were white, and they don't like that some people aren't?

"Five."

Daniel was sweating.

His suit felt tight.

He missed his gun.

"Four."

Please please please please please...

Don't let her die...

Give yourself up, Sullivan, you deserve this fate more than her...

"Three."

Three?

Shit.

"Two."

Daniel looked into Wendy's eyes. She looked back. Beseeching him for help that he couldn't give.

"One."

"Fine!"

Sullivan stepped out, his hands in the air.

"Fine, I'm here!"

And, just as Daniel breathed a sigh of relief, Curtis said, "I'd already made it to one," and shot a bullet through Wendy's skull.

# CHAPTER THIRTY-FOUR

"NO!" SULLIVAN CRIED AS AN INNOCENT WOMAN'S BODY dropped to the ground.

"Just stop!" Sullivan shouted before Curtis could shoot another hostage. Even Walter appeared shocked at what Curtis had just done. This man was out of control.

Curtis turned his gun toward Sullivan.

Sullivan slowed down his heart. And his thoughts. Processed all the information...

"You don't need to kill anyone else," he said.

Curtis's finger stroked the trigger.

"It's enough, you have me," Sullivan persisted, but it wasn't enough, and he managed to return to the cover of the corridor as Curtis's gunshot hit the wall behind him.

"Get him!" Walter shouted at Curtis and Herman. "I'm fine here—get Sullivan!" Two sets of feet charged across the room.

Sullivan ran down the corridor as a few bullets hit the wall behind him. He entered the stairwell and leapt up the steps, taking them two at a time, thinking *shit* and *fuck* and *goddammit I could have saved that woman's life*.

He wasn't sure how he could have saved her life, but he was positive it was his fault.

Maybe if he'd have given himself up sooner?

*Then I'd be dead, and I won't be able to help the other hostages.*

Maybe if he'd have spoken more, perhaps talked Curtis down, processed things with him, made it sound like they were friends...

*You're clutching at straws.*

He knew it. Damn, even the hostages knew it.

But it didn't make that dead woman any more alive.

He passed a few rooms. Footsteps pounded up the stairs after him. He ducked into the nearest room and hid behind the door.

The sound of the door to the stairwell swinging preceded the stomps of Curtis and his lackies marching down the corridor. They sounded more reckless this time, almost too eager to find him. This was both advantageous and tricky; they would be less controlled, but more aggressive.

He could take down one of them, but then the other would open fire.

He just had to hope the one he killed was Curtis.

He held his breath. Listened. Clutched the handle of his knife.

Footsteps passed the room.

Sullivan barged open the door, grabbed the collar of the first man, and stuck the blade into his neck as he pushed him into the room opposite.

He pulled the door closed. Turned the lock.

Looked down at the man clutching his bleeding neck at Sullivan's feet.

It wasn't Curtis. It was the other one.

"Fuck!"

He took the man's gun from him. Considered putting the man out of his misery. He was suffering hard.

Then again, why should he?

The door handle turned, but it would not open.

Sullivan checked the ammunition in the dying man's gun. He had barely fired any bullets. Most of the gunfire must have come from Curtis.

Sullivan wondered how much this man had known about who he was fraternising with, and what they planned to do. Perhaps he thought they'd take a few hostages, make a few demands, and gain the admiration of all the other white supremacists.

Did he really not know how this was going to go down?

Then the man was a fool. Men like Curtis don't follow plans. Walter might think he was in charge; but Curtis would think otherwise.

The man stopped grabbing at his neck, and his body fell limp. His face fell into that same vacant, wide-eyed expression the other corpses had.

Sullivan hadn't even noticed there was another body slumped on an office chair behind him.

The shakes of the door stopped, and Sullivan wondered if Curtis was growing tired of trying to gain entry.

Then the gunshots started. Three bullets against the door lock to open it. Then a boot against the door to kick it open.

Sullivan lifted the gun into the air and shot. Curtis ducked around the door. A hole in the opposite wall told Sullivan that he'd missed. The sound of Curtis's heavy breathing told him the bastard was still there.

Curtis's foot was tapping. He was huffing. This prick was furious.

"What do you want?" Sullivan demanded.

He kept his gun aimed at the doorway, ready to pull the trigger as soon as he saw movement. He wasn't getting into another standoff. Sullivan was ready to blow this guy's head off.

What kind of sick fucker kills an innocent woman like that?

As the question passed through his thoughts, Sullivan tried not to think of the things he'd once done to people he didn't realise were innocent.

"I said what do you want?" Sullivan shouted.

The heavy breathing grew lighter. The foot stopped tapping. The huffs ceased.

And a slow, guttural chuckle, quiet and deliberate, incensed Sullivan further.

"You think you're saving the white race, is that it?"

No reply.

"Well, don't. We don't need any favours. I'm fairly sure the white guy is doing pretty well."

"Well, not anymore..."

His voice was singsong, like a demented clown; everything about this guy was insane.

"Not anymore?"

"Since you let them come and take that power..."

"Take that power? Look around—most rich people are white, most bosses are white, most cops are white—what *bloody power?*"

Sullivan reminded himself to calm down.

There was no reasoning with this man.

There would be no rational debate, and no enlightenment, and no newfound logic—it would be the same propaganda, the same nonsense they repeated to each other at their little meetings.

Truth was, Sullivan was quite apathetic with most people —no one affected him enough to make him like them or dislike him. Other people were just passengers on the train to death. But when it came to dickheads like Curtis, Sullivan loathed them. He'd never had a problem with an immigrant in his life. Honestly, they'd probably treated him better than anyone. Even if they were trying to gain power, as Curtis claimed—which Sullivan was sure they weren't—they'd make the world a better place if they did. After all, if the choice was to follow Curtis, he'd always choose the alternative.

"You know..." Curtis grumbled. "I thought... You were... Some kind of legend..."

"Yeah, I thought that once, too."

"But you couldn't even save that woman from dying."

Sullivan almost pulled the trigger, but forced self-restraint.

"I'm going to kill you," Sullivan murmured.

"What was that?"

"I said I'm going to kill you. Either now, when you come around that door, or when I catch you. I will, I swear."

"You didn't even know the woman. What with all the people you've killed, surely it's just one more..."

"I killed because my government taught me it was right, then I realised I was wrong. When are you going to have your awakening?"

Curtis forced an audible yawn.

"Bored now," he said, and Sullivan heard the click of a lighter.

# CHAPTER THIRTY-FIVE

JAY SULLIVAN WAS GETTING TIRESOME.

If Curtis wanted a lecture, he'd ring his parents.

Right now, he wanted blood.

So Curtis decided to end it.

A door beside Curtis led to a kitchen. Silently, he backed into it, unnoticed by Sullivan, and searched the drawers until he found what he was after.

Whiskey. That was the beautiful thing about strong booze – it was both tasty and flammable.

"You know…" he mused, as he returned to the corridor, tucking his gun behind his belt and opening his lighter. "This is a real shame. In another life, we could have had a beer and shared war stories."

"The only war you know is the one you created. You're scum."

They were just words, and they melded into nothingness. Curtis was preoccupied by the whisky that he held in front of his face. He unscrewed the lid. He placed it beneath his nose, smelt its beauty, and wished he would be around to hear Sullivan's screams as he burnt to death.

That's when he realised Sullivan was still talking.

"—and there is another way, if you are just willing to—"

"Stop, please, stop, just... stop."

"We could still have that beer."

"Oh, really?"

"Yeah. Put down the gun. I'll put down mine. Then we can walk out now, to the local, and have a pint."

Curtis considered telling Sullivan that he'd put his gun away a while ago. Instead, he sighed, and thought about what a fool Sullivan believed him to be.

"And what, we'll just forget all the people I've killed today?"

"If I can forget my kills, then maybe I can forget yours."

"And the FBI – are they going to let us stroll out of here?"

"I'll find another way out."

"There is no other way out. Besides, we have bigger plans."

He scanned the doorway. Considered how best to distribute the alcohol. Did he wave it around and splash the fluid about, or did he throw it in the room with the lighter and hope the two met?

"Bigger plans? What bigger plans?"

"You know that black FBI man... I forget his name..."

"Daniel Winstead."

"Fuck me, that was quick. How'd you know his name, you humping them now?"

"What do you mean by *them*?"

Curtis laughed. It really was like he was talking to his mother.

"Is a tough guy like yourself scared of a few letters?"

Sullivan didn't reply.

"Well, I hope you've said your goodbyes."

"What, you're going to shoot him?"

"Nah ah ah, wrong again."

"Then what?"

"You ever heard of the White House?"

"Yes, I know the bloody White House."

"You know what an effigy is?"

"Yes. Why?"

"Goodbye, Sullivan."

"Hang on, what? What are you going to–"

Curtis splashed the whisky over the doorway, then threw the bottle into the room.

Sullivan shot the gun, but Curtis was already backing away.

He held the lighter before him, lined the flame up with the doorway, and took aim.

"What are you–"

Curtis threw the lighter, and the doorway was immediately ablaze, blocking Sullivan's exit from the office.

Its heat reached out for Curtis as its chaos danced back and forth. It was a destructive beauty, pirouetting about like a demented ballerina. If the fire was a woman, he'd fuck it.

Sullivan was shouting something, but Curtis couldn't even hear him anymore.

Regretting that he couldn't stay to witness Sullivan scream, Curtis made his way back to the hostages, ready for the big finale.

# CHAPTER THIRTY-SIX

WENDY'S LIFELESS FACE REMAINED VISIBLE FOR ALL THE hostages to see. As if deliberate. As if to say to them—*this is what could happen.*

Daniel stood still. His arms were aching from keeping his hands on his head. But it didn't matter. Not when the dead body of Wendy lay staring at him, her dress riding up her lifeless legs. He'd seen plenty of dead bodies, but he rarely saw a corpse he knew.

Wendy was a lovely woman. A caring mother. A hard worker. Always keen to make someone's day just that bit brighter.

And now she was dead.

For what?

These white supremacists had killed a lot of white people to apparently defend the white race. Their ideology was fucked.

Daniel felt eyes on him. He turned. Berkley was staring at him. From his place on the floor, hands on the back of his head, Berkley was trying to get Daniel's attention.

When he finally did, Berkley nodded his head toward Walter.

Walter was on his own. With his back turned to Berkley. In the middle of a conversation with someone on the phone. Someone within their group, perhaps. Ranting about the fuck-ups, and Jay Sullivan, and frequently mentioning something about a yacht. As he spoke, he waved his gun around without a care for its power, gesticulating like you would with a pen or a cigarette. As if it was nothing, and not an instrument of death. The careless way he held his weapon suggested that he had no formal training. These people were not organised, militant terrorists—they were opportunists. Home-grown idiots. People who could fire a weapon, but couldn't produce a thorough plan.

This was clear by Walter leaving his spare gun on the desk next to him.

Daniel met Berkley's eyes and gave him a gentle nod. He knew Berkley well; he'd overseen Berkley's training himself. Walter was engrossed in his thoughts, and this gave Berkley opportunity to sneak up on him, take the gun that had been dim-wittedly discarded on the counter and shoot him.

Daniel had full confidence in Berkley's ability to do this. He had to. It was probably their only chance.

Berkley surveyed the room. What was the best route? He was at the edge of the hostages, so he was probably better off going around the perimeter of the silently whimpering bodies.

Daniel shared a look with Berkley. He raised his eyebrows as if to warn that he should take caution, then gave a subtle nod to indicate that Berkley should proceed.

Berkley peered at the back of Walter's head, waiting for Walter to notice him.

He didn't. Walter was too immersed in his conversation.

Berkley cricked his neck, closed his eyes for a moment of

prayer, then began crawling along the ground. Another hostage saw what Berkley was doing and looked on the verge of panic. Berkley placed a finger over his mouth, then lowered his hand as a sign for this man to return to his dormant position; which he did.

Berkley continued around the edge of the captives, close enough that, should Walter turn around, he could return to the cluster of hostages and remain unnoticed.

Daniel held his breath.

These were the moments they trained for, but never expected to happen; these were the moments where training meant nothing, and instinct proved everything.

Berkley crept around the perimeter, keeping his eyes focussed on Walter.

Walter, completely oblivious, was ranting about more crap —immigrants yada yada stealing our power yada yada superiority yada yada – it was nothing different to what people without a purpose have been purporting for decades.

Berkley was only metres away. He was so close.

Daniel turned to Walter, focussed on his eyes, looking for a flicker of a sixth sense, an unconscious awareness that someone was sneaking up on him—but there was none. When this man started talking about his beliefs, he did not stop.

Berkley approached Walter, moving like a spider, legs then arms, and turned his focus to the gun on the counter.

Walter turned, as if about to face Berkley, and both Daniel and Berkley tensed—then Walter threw out his arm as he shouted something at his friend, and turned back again, completely unaware.

Daniel saw the relief spread across Berkley's face.

Berkley crept closer, until he was just behind Walter, and reached for the gun.

Walter turned, and Berkley had to retract his arm. Walter

continued with his conversation, making plans with this yacht he kept mentioning, and Berkley reached his arm out again.

Then the fire alarm went off.

"What the fuck?" Walter said, looking upwards.

Berkley was too committed now. He was away from the hostages and could not sink back in with them unnoticed.

He leapt toward the gun, just as the ominous figure of Curtis appeared beside Daniel. Berkley's fingers only just grasped the handle as Curtis fired a bullet through his torso.

"No..." Daniel stifled his scream so it was just a whimper. He could not stop staring at his colleague. He fell to his knees, with no control over his body. It made little sense at first. How was Berkley alive a second ago, but so still now?

"That fucker was creeping up on you, by the way." Curtis said. "What's happening with the yacht?"

"He's letting us use it."

"Was he impressed when he'd seen what we've done?"

"Ecstatic."

Their words faded to background noise. Like they were underwater. Daniel couldn't decipher a word.

All he could see was Berkley's face, with not a flicker of movement on it.

How had Berkley been so close; he'd held the gun in his hand; he was about to shoot Walter, and now he was so... Dead...

"Is Sullivan dead?" Walter asked Curtis.

"Good as."

"Where's Herman?"

"Dead."

"Fuck!" Walter punched the desk. "What's with the fire alarm?"

"I had to set the place on fire. It's time to go."

Walter turned to the crowd of hostages and fired his gun into the air.

"Right, ladies and gents—it's time to go! Any of you break rank, and I'll put a fucking bullet in your head! Now get up, all of you."

The hostages rose to their feet as Walter took his place behind them.

Curtis, however, did not join Walter. Instead, he approached Daniel, looking down at the FBI agent who was still on his knees, still staring at Berkley.

"Right," Curtis said. "We have a different plan for you."

"Go to hell."

Curtis struck the butt of the gun across Daniel's temple, forcing him to the floor.

He crouched beside Daniel, pressing the barrel of the gun at the base of his skull, and speaking slowly and sadistically into his ear.

"I will shoot you in places that will hurt you very, very badly if you talk to me like that again. You understand?"

Daniel contemplated another retort. He stayed silent.

"You are beneath me. You are not to even fucking look at me.

Daniel shook his head. Scrunched up his face. Held in all his anger. Thought of his children growing up without a father.

"Get up."

Curtis dragged Daniel to his feet, and Daniel let him. With the gun against the back of his head, Curtis guided Daniel out behind the other hostages.

# CHAPTER THIRTY-SEVEN

THE DOORS OPENED, AND THE HOSTAGES SHUFFLED OUT.

Curtis licked his lips. Oh boy, how this excited him.

Police cars and black cars surrounded the building. Police officers and FBI agents with their bullet-proof vests focussed their guns on the innocent civilians being guided out.

Behind them, Walter kept his gun aimed at the hostages' heads, remaining among them, sure that they wouldn't dare fire a gun if it jeopardised the life of a civilian. Curtis followed, holding onto Daniel's collar with one hand, and pressing the gun against Daniel's head with the other.

Above them, smoke came from the windows, fire raging against the glass.

"Drop your guns!" shouted Walter. "Drop them, or we'll kill another hostage!"

He grabbed the collar of a nearby hostage and pressed the gun against his temple, demonstrating what they would risk with non-compliance.

"Do it now!"

An FBI agent lifted his gun, placed it on the ground, and

indicated at everyone else to do the same. All police and FBI agents followed.

"Now kick them away."

The lead agent obeyed by kicking his gun away. Everyone else reluctantly followed. Curtis did an excitable little jig.

"We have done what you asked," the man said. "Now, will you let them go?"

"Now the snipers!"

The man hesitated.

"I said the fucking snipers – lose them or we'll shoot!"

The man sighed, a pained expression conveying his disappointment. As he stared from the faces of one vulnerable hostage to another, he picked up his radio, and gave the instruction. Up above, figures on the top of nearby rooftops backed away.

"Satisfied?" the man asked.

Curtis dragged Daniel toward their car, just a few steps away. They kept instructing the hostages to stay close, ensuring they were always surrounded. They didn't trust the FBI; if any of them had the opportunity to pick up one of their guns and shoot, they'd take it, and it was important they kept their collateral close.

"Move," he instructed, pointing his gun at each of them. "Now."

The agents, with their hands in the air, could only watch as Curtis, Walter and Daniel moved closer to their car.

"Keep going..."

Curtis noticed a pair of handcuffs on an officer's belt. The guy was standing in front of his car, glaring at them.

"Throw me your handcuffs," Curtis instructed.

The man hesitated.

Curtis cocked his gun and pressed it harder against Daniel's head. Walter put his gun against a hostage's head, forcing a pathetic whimper from the random woman.

"Now!" Curtis growled.

The officer threw his handcuffs toward Curtis, and they landed at Daniel's feel.

"Put them on," Curtis instructed Daniel.

With a sigh, and a moment of contemplation where he ran through his options, Daniel took the cuffs and went to put them on.

"No—behind your back," Curtis instructed.

Daniel did as he was told.

"Get in the back of the car."

He climbed into the back of the car. Curtis remained by the open door, his gun pointed at the hostages, still keeping them close.

"All of you," Curtis said at the agents and cops around the nearby cars. "Move away from your vehicles, or my man shoots a hostage."

They obeyed.

Curtis nodded at Walter.

He threw himself onto the backseat beside Daniel, and Walter took to the driver's seat. He hit the gas and sped across the road, forcing police to dive out of the way.

He swung around corners, narrowly missing pedestrians, mounting the kerb to cut the right turn. He reached a line of police cars who'd placed spikes across the road. He mounted the kerb again and drove over the sidewalk to avoid them, narrowly missing the police officers and completely missing the spikes.

The cops didn't fire at them. They had evidently been advised not to. It was the advantage of having a hostage.

Walter looked in the rear-view mirror at Curtis, who grinned—then at Daniel, who glared.

"We're almost there," Walter said.

"Fucking-a," Curtis said with glee, and placed his gun

against Daniel's head. "And you do not move—we haven't got long to go now."

Curtis was shaking, fuelled with adrenaline and excitement. He thoroughly believed they'd gotten away and were on route to Washington with no one to stop them.

Which was why, as Curtis leant back, revelling in their success, he was surprised to hear police sirens.

# CHAPTER THIRTY-EIGHT

THE CORRIDOR FILLED WITH FIRE. ITS FLAMES REACHED FOR Sullivan, trying to catch his body in its grip.

But it didn't spread any further than the doorway.

At least Curtis was stupid enough not to realise that fire would not spread over a marble floor. The fire itself was reduced to the space in which Curtis had spread the alcohol.

But it was still blocking his exit down the corridor.

Outside the office window, Sullivan could hear shouting. He looked outside. There was a side street below, with a few dumpsters but otherwise empty. If he stretched, he could just about make out the street to his right where one could access the front of the embassy; there appeared to be a commotion.

He heard Walter shout something, then the police and FBI agents dropped their guns.

Why were they dropping their guns?

*Because they are letting them get away...*

Sullivan sighed. Dropped his head. Lamented their poor decision. But it wasn't his problem now; the FBI and the cops would do their best to protect these people. If he could leave and avoid being captured, then that was his best option.

Except, he still couldn't quell the nagging doubt that he could do better than the FBI. Not just because of his higher level of training and experience—albeit, he wasn't the proficient warrior he used to be—but because their rules did not constrain him. There was no procedure he needed to follow. There were no ethics he'd have to worry about. He wasn't concerned about his media image.

But all he'd done so far was cause the death of a hostage. Sure, he'd taken out a few of the terrorists—but what good had that done?

Enough. It was time for him to go.

He opened the window. There was a fire escape further along the wall; he'd noticed it when he was on the roof.

He sat on the window ledge and turned his legs around so they were dangling out. Everyone below was so preoccupied with the drastic scenes of Walter and Curtis's escape at the front of the building that he managed to climb onto the ledge without being noticed.

Then came the leap to the fire escape.

Fifteen years ago, he wouldn't have even hesitated.

Now, he couldn't help feeling he was incredibly stupid for even trying it.

"What are you doing..." he muttered to himself.

He crouched on the ledge, ignored the sensible thoughts telling him not to do this, and used his aching knees to push himself off. He dropped a little too much, but managed to catch the lower rungs of the ladder. He swung his body upwards, placed his legs on the ladder, and mentally congratulated himself on surviving. He ascended the ladder, reaching the roof, and climbed up. From here, he could look down at the scene below with a perfect view.

The cops and agents had discarded their guns, and Walter and Curtis were backing away from the hostages.

Sullivan was about to consider the best route to the airport when he noticed a hostage who hadn't escaped.

Daniel Winstead. Forced to handcuff his own hands behind his back and shoved into the car.

Sullivan bowed his head.

They were about to get away with this FBI agent.

This FBI agent who'd hunted and arrested Sullivan.

This FBI agent who'd gloated about the potential of Sullivan getting the death penalty.

This FBI agent who thought of Sullivan as a piece of shit.

But, unlike the FBI, Sullivan knew what they planned to do with him.

They would set Daniel alight outside The White House. To make an example of him. To show the power of white superiority, and to further oppress the black community.

At best, this would be a tragic way to die. At worst, racial tensions would increase, and the race war so many racists had declared imminent would arrive.

Not only would Daniel experience an agonising death, but the action could destroy any stability and peace between the races this country had established. It would give way for closet racists to emerge from the shadows. It would give power to their movement.

Letting this happen would be an immense danger to society.

Sullivan sighed. Bowed his head.

This wasn't up to him, dammit.

This wasn't his fight.

He didn't care about *society*.

He was a nomad, left to live life alone. Hoping to see his estranged daughter again one day. Travelling the world without being noticed. Getting angry at memories of his father.

His father, the hero police officer who put people in cells

just because they were black. This police officer who tainted the image of all police officers with his abhorrent beliefs. His father, who would forever be a stain on Sullivan's character.

If someone had the chance to stop his father, they would have saved both Sullivan, and the people Sullivan ended up killing. The anger the government had used to turn him into their pawn would not have existed, he wouldn't have become an assassin, and they would have spared the world a lot of pain.

By stopping Walter and Curtis, did he have the chance to stop another child growing up like him? And then, of course, there was Daniel, soon to be put to a horrific death.

"Fuck!" he growled. He wanted to leave. He needed to leave. He didn't owe anyone anything.

*So why the bloody hesitation?*

The car drove away.

They were going to escape.

Other cars followed, but kept their distance. They'd have set up a perimeter to stop Walter and Curtis escaping, but what if Walter and Curtis got past it? Then what?

The authorities would pursue their targets for as long as it was safe; if that chase endangered the public, then it would be called off.

No one would ever call Jay Sullivan off, and that was the advantage he had.

Once again, it was up to him. The man who tried to avoid killing people, but always seemed to return to being a master of death.

He hated this life. The circumstance. The abilities.

He wanted a drink.

He wanted to sit in a bar until the barman kicked him out for being too drunk. He wanted to disappear to a third-world country where he wouldn't be found. He wanted to sleep with a whore, then never have to see her again.

Yet here he was.

The conscience he'd rejected for so many years pulling at his body.

He couldn't run away even if he wanted to.

He returned to the fire escape, hurried down, and searched the nearby streets for a vehicle. Some agents were entering the building, about to discover bodies. Most were pursuing the terrorists.

Sullivan ran toward a civilian starting his motorbike on an adjacent street.

"I need that," Sullivan said, appearing behind him.

The man scoffed and turned back away from him.

"I really need that."

"Eh, fuck off, would you?"

Sullivan, instantly regretting it, punched the man in the face and knocked him to the floor. A few people walking past screamed in surprise. There were enough people here to make sure he didn't have a concussion. The man would be fine.

Sullivan mounted the motorbike, twisted the handle, and sped toward the sound of the sirens.

# CHAPTER THIRTY-NINE

It didn't take long until Sullivan was on the highway, amongst a mass of police cars and black cars. Sirens blared, forcing civilians to pull their cars to the inside lane. He could just about make out Walter and Curtis's car in the distance.

Sullivan hung back, hoping that the authorities would deal with these two lunatics so he wouldn't have to.

The motorbike itself was a BMW S1000R—a 2021 model, still shiny and new, and he almost felt bad about robbing what must be an expensive bike from a man who'd had to work hard for it. If he could, he would leave it somewhere to be discovered, and hopefully returned. It drove beautifully, gliding side to side as he interweaved through cars at a speed that would kill him if he made a false move. It was a light bike; a slick model that was perfect for pursuit.

Walter seemed to slow the car down, and Sullivan wondered if this was their surrender. But of course it wasn't. It was simply allowing for Curtis to open the window and aim his AK-47 at the cars in pursuit.

They slowed down and backed off, but could not prevent themselves from being sprayed by a stream of bullets.

Curtis, noticing the authorities were retreating, aimed the gun at civilians pulling their cars to the side of the road, smashing the windows and leaving holes in the cars.

Sullivan knew exactly what would happen next.

The police and the FBI would decide it was too risky. That they couldn't put civilians in danger. And the only way to do this would be to end the pursuit, hoping this meant Curtis would stop firing.

And that was just what they did.

They slowed down and pulled over to the side of the road; every police and FBI vehicle backing off their targets.

Even the helicopter that hovered overhead, keeping track of their movements, did not escape being the target of Curtis's liberal gunshots. He fired up at the helicopter, even clipping its landing skids.

Inevitably, the helicopter retreated too.

Leaving them free to escape.

But Sullivan did not cease his pursuit—though he did not engage either. He remained at a distance, keeping sight of them, but doing so by hanging back, tracking their movements by the cars that had twisted to the side to avoid collision.

He pursued them over Bayonne Bridge and entered Staten Island. He followed the carnage through Elm Park, past Staten Island Zoo, and toward Fox Hills.

They must be heading for the harbour.

Sullivan slowed down, sure that Curtis and Walter were approaching their target destination. Once he was under the speed limit, he drove over Hylan Boulevard, and approached the harbour, where he saw the car.

Sullivan left the motorbike at the side of the road and crept toward the car. It was empty. The doors still open, the keys in the ignition. They were not planning on returning to it. He searched inside of it, unable to find any weapons, and assumed they had taken them with them.

From the car, he crept toward the harbour and hid behind a fence.

There were a few boats Sullivan assessed. Two didn't look like they were going anywhere. Another had a man on it, sitting next to a teenage boy and a set of fishing gear.

Then there was a yacht. Large and expensive. It could easily be 70 metres in length and had three decks with more space below. It looked more like a party ship heading to Ibiza than a getaway boat. Sullivan had heard of these white supremacy groups being the street fighters for benefactors who were far, far richer than them—this was an expensive yacht, the kind supplied by someone who believed in the cause, but didn't want to get their hands dirty. A businessman, or perhaps a politician. Someone with enough money to buy this boat without it denting the bank.

He scanned the area, and it didn't take long until he saw Curtis and Walter approaching the yacht. Curtis had his gun against Daniel's head and was pushing him forward. As they approached, they were greeted with cheers. There were plenty more of them on the boat, all skinheads, with the same swastika tattoos and Doc Martens, white t-shirts and pale blue jeans. From here, Sullivan couldn't tell how many there were, but there were enough to cause him a problem.

They shoved Daniel aboard, and the lemmings all gathered around him, making monkey noises and slapping his face and pushing him back and forth. They were playing with him like a predator might play with its food.

But they weren't predators. They were sheep. And they wouldn't be too difficult to take out.

They took Daniel inside, and the gang followed, ready to play with their food some more. After a minute or so, they appeared on the sky lounge deck at the top of the yacht. They shoved the beaten and bruised hostage to the floor and sat in a circle around him. Most sat back on sun loungers, but Curtis didn't—he sat on the edge of his, keeping his gun focussed on Daniel, ensuring that, at any moment, their hostage might contemplate fleeing, he would know how close he was to death.

Sullivan used this distraction to climb aboard unnoticed. He ran, hard and fast—as much as the fatigue caused by the day's exertions would allow him—until he reached the yacht.

He crept aboard at the stern, staying out of sight from a group of scumbags hanging around port side.

He entered the main deck. The sound of cheering from above had become fainter. He heard people talking around the corner, so he stepped lightly to the stairs and descended to the lower deck until he was as deep into the yacht as he could go.

He found a few toilets. He went inside one and locked the door. Took a few deep breaths.

He didn't want to take any more lives, but he had no choice. Everyone on this boat would have to die if Sullivan was to get to their hostage. He'd have to hope that Curtis and Walter were so determined to keep Daniel alive for when they reached Washington that they wouldn't execute him upon hearing the commotion.

He waited until the ship started moving. It took ten minutes, and he spent it convincing himself it was okay for him to do what he must. Resigned to another day of killing.

Dozens of lives to save one... it didn't seem a fair balance, somehow. Then again, sacrificing dozens of racist, ignorant scumbags to save a man trying to keep this world safe felt like a fair trade.

Daniel had arrested Sullivan because he believed it was the right thing to do—just as Sullivan had been his government's killer for the same reason. Daniel's life was worth more than theirs.

Still, Sullivan knew that some scumbags on this boat would be young. Had probably just become an adult. Still with the potential to learn the error of their ways. It would feel better if they were old and stubborn, rather than young enough that they could still be saved from their wayward ideology.

Either way, they were keeping an innocent man hostage, and were planning to set him alight in the name of white supremacy outside the most famous building in America.

Sullivan had no choice.

They were all going to die.

And, as the yacht left the harbour on course for Washington, he readied his knife, focussed his mind, and prepared for war.

# CHAPTER FORTY

ALONG THE SHORT CORRIDOR FROM THE BATHROOM, AND down the polished wooden floor of the lower deck, two skinheads sat together on a pristine leather sofa. The first used a credit card to separate strips of white powder, whilst the other ranted about his parents.

The first one had his back to Sullivan. The other didn't. Which meant surprise would not work. He'd have to try speed instead.

Sullivan strode along the corridor. The second one noticed him first, and went to grab his gun—but, in the time it took to aim, Sullivan had leapt onto the back of the sofa, then dived onto his opponent with his knife raised, and brought it down upon the fucker's neck.

As the other stood—not producing a weapon, so probably intending to run—Sullivan upturned the table so it landed on the guy's shin. Cocaine covered the carpet. Sullivan held his arm back and shoved the knife into the druggie's gut, before retracting it and swiping it across the guy's neck.

Two bodies by his feet and blood trickled off his knife.

Just like old times.

He ran to the stairs. There was a main deck, an upper deck, and a sky lounge deck still to go—Daniel was most likely to be located at the latter. He would have to take them out one by one.

He went up a few steps and paused, surveying the main deck. A glass bar with half-empty pint glasses took up a small section of the near wall. Beyond that, a large coffee table filled the space between a rectangle made of sofas. The sofas were white, ready to be stained red, and the cushions were burgundy and brown. Each wall had a window that gave way to the glorious sight of clear blue water and the skyline of New York. Beyond the sofas was a circular, brown polished table and four chairs.

Also in this room were another group of white suprema-cists. Four sat around the table playing poker. Four sat on the sofas—one with a mohawk, one with large, spiky hair that must be held in place by glue, one with a shaved head, and the last one who was older than the others, wearing a suit rather than the normal regalia of white t-shirts, braces, blue jeans and Doc Martens. Sullivan assumed the last guy was the one who owned the yacht. He looked smarmy and rich; the kind of guy most people would love to punch in the face.

Well, can't wait around; here goes.

Sullivan ran from his cover, dove to his knees, and brought his knife down on Mohawk's leg, leaving it in there. He took the handle of a pint glass, smashed it on the coffee table, and brought the biggest shard into the base of Spiky's throat as he attempted to stand. Sullivan removed the knife from Mohawk's leg, stuck it in and out of Mohawk's throat, then turned to face the others.

The guys playing poker had fled, no doubt to let Walter and Curtis know what was happening.

Older Guy had taken out a gun and was readying his aim. Sullivan lifted the coffee table and threw it at Older Guy, sending him off balance long enough for Sullivan to deal with the other two.

Skinhead was turning to run, so Sullivan skidded along his knees and stuck the knife in the back of skinhead's heel, forcing him to the floor, thus allowing him to turn to Spiky and shove the knife into the underside of his chin.

Older Guy had regathered himself, and was caught between fighting and fleeing. Sullivan lunged his knife at him, but he dodged it and lifted his gun. Sullivan lunged the knife again, forcing Older Guy to step out of its reach, allowing Sullivan to keep swinging the blade into the gun wielding hand. Older Guy cried out and dropped the gun. Sullivan pulled out the knife, a splatter of blood landing over his shoes, and stuck the knife in Older Guy's throat.

He turned back to Skinhead, who was trying to crawl away. Sullivan leapt upon him and dug the knife into his back.

Sullivan marched on, passing through the room and reaching the outside steps, which led him to the upper deck.

A stream of bullets fired at him the moment he reached the top step, forcing him to duck back around the corner.

He returned down the steps and concealed himself in a cupboard. The four guys who had previously played poker ran down the steps with their guns, passing Sullivan's hiding spot, and returned to the main deck.

Sullivan returned to the interior, ran up behind them and, as he engaged them in combat, he ensured he kept them in close proximity. This way, none of them could lift their gun without him blocking it. In one swift movement, he stuck the knife in the throat of the first guy, ducked a punch from the second guy, stuck a knife in his gut, took hold of the third guy's hand and fired his weapon at the fourth guy's leg, slit the fourth guy's throat, then finished with his knife in the third guy's gut.

He ran up the steps and out of sight. Paused. Damn, he was out of breath.

He used to do this kind of shit without breaking a sweat —now he was heaving.

His former mentor in the Falcons, as corrupt as he was, had taught Sullivan a valuable lesson: your mind has more control than your body. He only felt fatigued if he allowed it.

The interior was clear. Evidently, anyone on this deck had fled upstairs for strength in numbers. He ran through, passing a long dinner table surrounded by low, comfortable chairs. A few open doors at the end of the room led to bedrooms. Sullivan checked each of them, and they were clear.

He ascended the steps to the sky lounge deck and was immediately engaged in combat by another group. He ducked their knifes and used his to dispose of each in quick succession, then proceeded past a jacuzzi and a few sun loungers. There was a final door, behind which he was sure he'd find Daniel. In the distance, he saw the coast. A peaceful suburbia that Walter and Curtis would have to cross to reach the White House.

Walter stepped out of the room, his AK-47 aimed at Sullivan, and fired.

Sullivan ducked back around the corner, returning to the steps. Walter did not stop firing, and the bullets impacted the wall Sullivan hid behind. This made Sullivan smile. A professional would save the ammunition. A professional would wait for the perfect moment. A professional would charge forward with their gun raised, waiting for the opportunity to hit their target. But Walter was an amateur, and for that, Sullivan was grateful. He kept firing, hoping the bullets would intimidate Sullivan, probably like he'd seen in the movies.

Sullivan simply had to wait for Walter to run out of ammunition. Which he did.

Once the bullets stopped, Sullivan made his move,

running from his cover as Walter released the magazine from the gun and slotted another in. By the time Walter had aimed his reloaded gun, Sullivan had landed a fist against Walter's wrist, which forced Walter to drop the gun overboard.

Sullivan swung his knife at Walter, who ducked. He swung it again, and Walter sidestepped, then stepped back.

Then Sullivan paused. Watched Walter, who stood steps away, watching back.

"You know you can't stop this," Walter said. "I'm in charge, and I–"

"You're not in charge."

Walter frowned. "I think you'll find I am."

"Curtis is in charge. You're just a lackey who gives others orders."

Walter's lip curled into a snarl. "Fuck you—Curtis respects me."

Sullivan snorted away a laugh. "Curtis respects no one. A guy like him is just in it for the anarchy. You are a means to an end."

"That is not true—I am–"

Sullivan lunged forward.

Walter looked down to find blood dribbling from a hole in his belly.

Sullivan had said exactly the right things to distract an immature mind, and was able to watch Walter fall to his knees, clutching his wound.

As he did, he thrust the knife forward again, this time landing it in the side of Walter's neck.

Walter fell onto his front. His body convulsed. Blood spread across the wooden deck.

In the distance, the coast appeared. They were minutes away from arriving, and time was running out.

Sullivan glared at the last door.

Curtis was behind that door, as Sullivan assumed Daniel would be, too.

He did not know how he'd save Daniel, just as he did not know how to get inside the mind of a madman like Curtis. He would rather take on another boatful of skinheads than take on a nutter like that.

But, as he always had, he proceeded without a plan, reassuring himself that, so far, he'd always found a way.

He tucked his knife into his sock. Lifted Walter's gun. Checked it was loaded.Paced his hand against the door handle, pushed down, aimed the gun, and nudged the door open, remaining behind the wall.

# WASHINGTON DC, US

# CHAPTER FORTY-ONE

YET AGAIN, SULLIVAN ENTERED A STANDOFF WITH THIS SICK madman.

Except, this time, whilst Sullivan pointed his gun at Curtis, Curtis's gun was trained on someone else.

Daniel Winstead. He looked stricken with fear. Tired from an afternoon of torment. Puzzled at the sight of Sullivan bursting in to save him.

"Let him go," Sullivan instructed. He didn't know why he bothered. Curtis was hardly going to obey his instruction. Perhaps it was more that if Sullivan gave Curtis the option to surrender and Curtis didn't take it, it would make him feel less bad about Curtis's death.

Then again, he had to be in the position to kill Curtis first —then he could contemplate remorse.

"Ah ah ah," Curtis said. "I don't think so."

"Just drop the gun, Curtis. Let this be over. Enough people have died."

"You think I care about Walter, lying out there? You think I care about any of them?"

"No, I don't. But I think you care about yourself."

Curtis chuckled, each inward laugh forcing another jolt from his body.

"I thought you would be better than this," he admitted. "I am disappointed."

"Honestly, that won't keep me up at night."

The yacht—of which Sullivan was suddenly aware there was no one at the helm—was almost at the coast.

"You won't kill him," Sullivan pointed out. "You need him."

"You think I can't find another black guy as soon as I get off this boat?"

"I don't think you could find another black FBI agent."

"I'm willing to compromise."

Sullivan did not utter another retort. Silence fell between them. The yacht entered the shallow depths of water beside the coast, slowing down before hitting a small, wooden pier. It idled on the surface, aimlessly travelling along the coastal path, nudging other boats.

Behind Daniel, Sullivan saw signs for the Martin Luther King Jr memorial, and considered how sad it was that the world was still no better than when the monument was created.

"We're going to get off this boat now," Curtis decided, evidently growing bored by the lack of conversation. "And you're going to stay on the boat."

"Not happening."

"You will stay on it, or I will kill him."

Sullivan met Daniel's eyes.

For a moment, something passed between them. Perhaps it was gratitude that Sullivan had at least tried—or perhaps Sullivan was seeing something that wasn't there. What he was sure of, however, was the resolve in Daniel's eyes. He'd had enough of the day's events, and he was prepared for what came next.

But that was probably because he didn't know what was coming next.

"You're a cretin," Sullivan said. "A piece of shit. The crap I step over."

Curtis stuck out his lip and pretended to sob. "Your words hurt so much."

"You make the rest of us look bad. Those of us who are trying to create a bridge between our privilege and their poverty."

"Is that so?" Curtis said as he backed away, toward the stairs. "Tell me, what is it you're doing to breach that gap?"

Sullivan's eyes narrowed. "This."

Curtis dragged Daniel down the stairs, a hand on his collar and a gun against the base of his skull. Sullivan kept following, a few steps away, his gun aimed at Curtis's head.

As Curtis reached the edge of the main deck, he turned back to Sullivan, dragging Daniel toward the harbour.

"If you leave this boat, I will shoot him," he stated.

Sullivan was tempted to still follow them. But he didn't. He watched as Curtis led Daniel off the boat and onto the coast. He considered taking the shot, but he couldn't risk missing; he had no choice but to watch Curtis drag Daniel onto land, up West Basin Drive, and shove him into the back of a van.

Soon, they were out of sight, and the yacht kept drifting. A luxurious, expensive item funded by a businessman who hated diversity but didn't have the muscle to spread his hate himself.

He saw his father in Curtis. Not the tattoos, or the overt psychopathy—his father was far more subtle—but the anger, the fury, and the stubborn belief that he was right.

It made him loathe Curtis even more.

And he would not let him hurt Daniel. FBI-meathead-jerk or not, this was a battle he refused to lose.

Sullivan waited another minute, ensuring that Curtis had gone. He placed the gun over his shoulder and dived off the boat, into the shallow water. He stood as soon as he was able, and trudged onto the grassy verge, his clothes heavy with water.

He crossed the road, onto another patch of grass, toward a set of trees. The Washington Monument was visible in the distance.

Sullivan noticed a man, halfway into his parked car, staring at him. He caught sight of himself in the window of the man's car. His clothes were drenched, and his face and clothes were covered in drabs of other people's blood.

He paused by this man, leant against the car, and caught his breath.

"Hey, er..." he said, trying to appear nonchalant, "could you point me toward the White House?"

The man looked Sullivan up and down.

"I've been through hell to come and see it."

As the man kept gawking, he slowly lifted his hand and pointed to his right.

"Cheers," Sullivan said, and trudged onwards.

## CHAPTER FORTY-TWO

STRIPPED. HANDCUFFED. HUMILIATED.

Curtis Oswald had taken society back by centuries.

Was this how Daniel's life would end? An honest FBI agent disgraced in public?

The back of the van was dark, and smelt of moisture, but he could still see Curtis's black eyes focussed on him. He could feel the lecherous grin, smell the body odour, detect the glee.

"So, this is what you wanted, huh?" Daniel grunted. His voice was gravelly and his throat was sore. Random parts of his limbs throbbed with pain. His naked body was cold, but this didn't bother him as much as the degradation he felt.

He could smell the kerosene. There were tubs of it along the other side of the van. And he knew where they were, and he could guess where they were heading.

"You gonna set me on fire, is that it?"

Silence. Daniel could feel Curtis's pleasure. It made him feel sick.

"Helter Skelter," declared Curtis.

"What?"

"It was what Charles Manson called the race war he believed was imminent."

"You know Charles Manson was crazy, right?"

"Most visionaries are."

The van came to a stop. Seconds went past where they held each other's gaze. Daniel was intent on channelling all of his hatred into his glare, but it only seemed to excite Curtis more. Eventually, the doors opened, and the sunlight shone bright against Daniel's eyes. A man Curtis had called Roger stood there, dressed in the same regalia.

"We're here," Roger said.

Tourists filled the streets outside the van. Daniel knew where he was. He'd been to the White House before. It was a street or so away. He was tempted to ask why they didn't park closer—but the security around the White House was tough, and they were probably trying to avoid it. Were they intending to walk him there in chains? How would they do that without being noticed? Maybe they'd dress like cops, then walk him to the White House like *he* was the criminal. Or did they have the audacity to walk him there as they were, and rely on the bystander effect to get there unopposed?

Roger and Curtis were in deep conversation. Perhaps that was what they were discussing now: the logistics of how Daniel was going to die.

Daniel also wondered whether his colleagues would have tracked them here. Then again, wouldn't they be here by now if they had?

And if they were searching for him, would they stretch their search as far as Washington?

Would Daniel?

He wasn't sure if he would. If you stretch the perimeter too far, you end up with a space that's too large to search.

"Are you ready to become a martyr?" Roger asked, cutting

through Daniel's thoughts as he stepped inside the back of the van.

Curtis sniggered. They opened the tubs of kerosene. Daniel considered struggling, but what would be the point? His hands were bound behind his back, adrenaline was running out, and fatigue was making every movement tough.

So he let them do what they wanted.

Feeling humiliated and pathetic, he let them.

They threw the contents of the tubs over him. His body stank. It reminded him of the diesel he put in the people carrier at home.

*At home.*

Where his wife was. With his children. Soon, they would see him on the news. One of his colleagues would arrive at their house to tell them of his death. He wondered if someone he knew would do it, or whether they'd choose someone who was emotionally detached from the case.

Curtis and Roger stepped out of the van and looked in at him. The sunlight made his kerosene-soaked body glisten.

"We ready to go?" Roger asked Curtis.

Curtis took out a box of matches. "Yes. Get him."

Roger went to drag Daniel out.

But he was interrupted by a voice, gruff and assertive, too loud to ignore: "Drop the fucking matches!"

The thought of salvation became a distant possibility as Daniel heard the last voice he thought he'd be grateful to hear.

He tried to peer out of the van, but he couldn't see.

Curtis grinned at someone. Held his hands in the air. But Sullivan could not stop Roger from launching himself into the back of the van and pressing the barrel of his gun against Daniel's head. The sun-kissed outline of Jay Sullivan appeared through the open doors. Sullivan looked in at Daniel, and in his eyes. Daniel realised just how awful he looked.

Sullivan tightened his grip on the gun he aimed at Curtis.

"Let him go."

"It's too late," Curtis said.

"Tell your man to take his gun off Daniel. It's over."

"It's far from over."

"Do it now!"

"Make me."

Curtis was right.

Sullivan couldn't shoot him; he might hit Daniel, and Sullivan will have failed.

"So this is what you do – hide behind your gun?" Sullivan said. "Can't face me properly?"

"You're holding a gun too."

Sullivan held his gun in the air, raised his eyebrows at Curtis, then threw his gun to the side.

"Come on, Curtis. You couldn't even beat me in a bar brawl. Why don't you face me properly?"

"You are a strange man."

"You got no gun, I got no gun. Fists to fists, Curtis. Let's see who's still standing."

Curtis opened his mouth in mocked shock, looked at Roger, then back to Sullivan.

"We really don't have time to—"

"You're too chickenshit to fight me, that why?"

"I've beaten you already! Over and over and over."

"Yet I keep coming back."

Curtis sighed. Rubbed his sinuses. "You are irritating."

"No guns. Just us. Come on. Let's see what you got. Or are you a coward?"

Curtis huffed. He looked resistant, but Daniel could tell Curtis was the kind of man who was vulnerable to insults against his ego. Sullivan had said the right things to lure him into a fight.

Only, Daniel wasn't sure it was a fight Sullivan could win.

And as far as civilians walking past would be concerned—these were just two idiots brawling in the street. No one could see Daniel being held captive. People might just keep walking and not even bother calling the cops. Which would suit Sullivan as well as Curtis; he didn't want to get caught either.

Either way, this was a terrible idea.

"Fine." Curtis nodded. Placed the matches in his pocket. Took the gun out from the back of his waist and threw it in the van. Discarded his jacket along with it.

Sullivan was either really smart—appealing to Curtis's ego, to Curtis's ideology, to his striving for the perfect image of white supremacy—or he was really stupid, and had just begun both of their death sentences.

Curtis stepped forward, his fists raised.

"Come on then," Curtis said. "Let's fuck shit up."

## CHAPTER FORTY-THREE

SULLIVAN HAD BRAWLED WITH DRUNKS ACROSS THE WORLD.

He'd brawled with white people, with black people, with Asian people.

He'd brawled with skinny people, fat people, people with biceps bigger than Sullivan's head, and people with extensive martial arts knowledge.

He'd brawled with nasty people, with abhorrent people, with calm and calculated people, and with mad people.

Out of all those that he'd brawled with, it was the mad that gave him the toughest fights. One can predict the move of a superb martial artist, as they would recreate the moves they'd practised so many times—but one cannot predict the next move of a man whose mind was so chaotic that he didn't even know what he was doing next.

Which was why Sullivan took more caution than he cared to admit. He backed away from Curtis as his opponent hunched his body, making it seem stockier somehow, and swung his first punch.

Sullivan blocked it, but Curtis did not stop swinging. From one side to the next, he threw his entire body weight behind each fist. He was a scraggly fucker, but he threw a hard punch.

Sullivan kept his head blocked, then ducked the tenth or eleventh swing and uppercut Curtis. This knocked Curtis back. Sullivan should have left it there and regrouped, but he was cocky, and he swung an elbow toward Curtis's chin.

Curtis dodged it and sunk his teeth into Sullivan's shoulder.

Sullivan cried out, and a few heads turned in their direction. He punched Curtis in the gut, over and over, even kneed him in the bollocks, but each strike just prompted Curtis to dig his teeth down harder.

Sullivan tried swinging Curtis off him, but Curtis wrapped his legs around Sullivan's waist. Blood trickled down his sleeve, hot and sticky. He turned toward the nearest brick wall and charged at it, hoping to slam Curtis's head into it. Curtis, however, dropped off Sullivan at the last moment, forcing Sullivan to charge himself into the wall.

The sky spun, and for the first time in this fight, he found himself on his back, staring up at the sky. A cloud passed by. It was shaped like a boulder. The momentary respite didn't last long as an elbow broke the sunny skies and dropped to Sullivan's face. He was alert enough to roll out of the way, and Curtis's elbow landed on the pavement.

This didn't deter Curtis. If anything, it spurred him on more. He mounted Sullivan and pounded his fists, one at a time, against the side of Sullivan's head, and the world grew dizzier.

It prompted a memory through his muddled mind.

He was a child. His mother cowered in the corner. His father was atop him. Throwing one fist, then the other. Just like then, and just like now, he failed to be rid of the racist beating the shit out of him.

A burst of fury sent adrenaline through his body. He

would not let his father beat him again. Or anyone. He struck his elbows against Curtis's knees and, in a jujitsu move he wasn't sure how he remembered, he lifted his waist and rolled over before Curtis could move his knees back. He rolled onto his back with Curtis beneath him, straddling him from behind. Sullivan stood, carrying the weight of Curtis with him, and dropped himself onto his back, hoping to strike Curtis against the ground—but Curtis dropped off, meaning Sullivan struck his own spine against the pavement.

He roared. Stood. Charged at Curtis and rugby tackled him, lifting him into the air and slamming him against the bonnet of the van.

Curtis shoved his fingers into the wound on Sullivan's shoulder. Sullivan hollered in pain. Curtis laughed.

The bastard was enjoying this.

Sullivan retracted an arm and aimed his fist at Curtis's knee. Curtis moved his leg out of the way, and Sullivan's knuckles pounded against the metal hood of the van, bruising his fingers and shedding his skin.

Sullivan pushed himself away from Curtis and stood back, gathering himself.

He surveyed his opponent. Barely bruised, as Sullivan stood there like a wreck.

This made him angrier.

But he couldn't be angry.

He had to be cool.

Or he stood no chance.

For a moment, he considered grabbing the gun Curtis had discarded in the van. Could he get there first? But then he remembered Roger's gun against Daniel's head. And he snarled, and with renewed vigour, he charged at Curtis, grabbing him by the neck and throwing him against a parking meter.

Curtis landed on his back and sprung back to his feet like

a dead chicken brought back to life, his limbs operating on a different level to his body.

Sullivan charged forward again, struck Curtis in the face, then struck again to find his punch dodged, and he stumbled forward.

He looked back at Curtis. Blood oozed from his lip. Curtis stuck his tongue out, licked the blood up, and smiled like he enjoyed it.

The sadistic sonofabitch.

Curtis stretched his arms. Bounced up and down. Ready for the next round.

And in the movements of Curtis's body, Sullivan recognised the erratic nature of fighting that seemed so familiar. The unpredictability, the aggression, the enjoyment of the violence. The nasty, racist pig. The ignorant piece of shit.

He saw his father looking back at him.

And for this, he hated Curtis even more.

And he charged at him, trying to take him to the ground, but missed, and was tripped up. Curtis mounted him, and this time countered the jujitsu move by pinning Sullivan's shoulders down.

Curtis placed his hands on Sullivan's throat and squeezed.

# CHAPTER FORTY-FOUR

ROGER WAS OLDER THAN MOST OF THEM. BUT HE WAS STILL an idiot. Daniel could see that. The way he held the gun... it was so untrained. There was no support with his spare hand. It was a man who had joined a cause because he wanted to be something better, and had become something worse.

They both strained to hear the commotion from the other side of the van. The grunts. The slams.

Roger kept his gun aimed at Daniel, but his gaze couldn't help floating toward the open doors.

Daniel watched him, then looked at Curtis's gun, a few steps away from Roger, that Curtis had discarded in the van.

If he could just grab that gun...

He was aching. Agonising. Tired. Devastated. His hands were bound behind him, and he was emotionally distraught, and hurting in every muscle he was consciously aware of.

But they were going to kill him, anyway. He may as well try something. He was sat in the back of a van, naked, covered in kerosene, waiting to burn to death; he had little to lose.

The thought itself filled him with enough renewed adrenaline to make his decision.

He looked at the gun. At Roger. The gun. Roger. The gun. Roger.

Which would he go for first?

He flexed his hands, ignoring the pain of the handcuffs around his wrists. He straightened his arms, flexing muscles he willed to work. He took a deep breath, let it out, and readied himself for a fight.

Without further thought or hesitation, he leapt from his place on the floor and charged his shoulder into Roger.

Roger yelped and dropped his gun. He stretched his arm out for it, but Daniel charged him again, shoved him against the corner of the van, then lifted his head back and brought his forehead down on Roger's nose. An audible crack coincided with the impact.

Roger fell to his knees, clutching his face.

Daniel lifted his foot and brought his heel down on Roger's head. His bare foot had less impact than a boot, and it took a few strikes until it disorientated Roger enough that he wouldn't get up.

At least not for a minute or two.

He wasn't completely knocked out, just groggy.

Daniel dropped his back onto Roger, pinning him down with all his body weight, and searched his pockets for the key to his handcuffs. Without being able to see what his hands were doing, he relied solely on the feel of objects, feeling his way to Roger's left pocket.

No keys.

Roger's eyes opened, blinked out the blood, and looked around. Daniel retracted his head and brought it down on Roger's nose again.

Daniel rolled over Roger's body and searched inside Roger's other pocket.

Still no keys.

He looked around the van, desperate for a solution. Then he found it. Curtis's discarded jacket. He grabbed it behind his back and searched for the feeling of the keys inside the pockets.

With a huge sigh of relief, he found them. Using the tips of his fingers, he felt for the key that fit in the handcuffs. As he did, he noticed Roger regathering himself, looking around, realising what had happened.

The gun was inches away from him.

Daniel twisted his wrists, putting the key in the handcuffs. But he didn't have time.

Roger was standing. And he was reaching for his gun.

Daniel pushed himself up and threw his body toward the gun, landing on his back so his hands could grab it. He felt for the trigger and, just as Roger took aim, Daniel twisted his body away from Roger and shot the gun several times in his direction.

A moment passed where Daniel was expecting to feel the pain of a bullet.

But he didn't.

He turned around, and Roger's body was slumped in the van's corner, a bullet wound in his thigh and his chest. His face was devoid of life.

Daniel tried again to unlock the handcuffs.

# CHAPTER FORTY-FIVE

"WHAT WAS THAT?"

Curtis looked over his shoulder at the sound of gunshots coming from the van, and this gave Sullivan the chance to throw a punch at his elbow and loosen Curtis's grip on his throat.

Sullivan gasped for breath.

"For fuck's sake!" Curtis shouted, resuming his throttling. "Just die!"

Faint sirens came from the distance.

"It looks like I don't have much time," Curtis said, growing tired at how long it takes to strangle a man to death.

Sullivan tried to push Curtis off, but Curtis struck him again, and his eyelids began to droop.

Curtis looked around. He sought a weapon. Something to end this. Anything.

He noticed a loose brick by the kerb. Part of the road that needed repair. He reached for it, wrapped his spindly fingers around it, and lifted it high above his head, ready to bring it down upon Sullivan's skull.

Sullivan tried pushing Curtis off, but his body failed him.

The strength he had at the beginning of this day—what little there was of it—had faded. His body was too tired. Too delayed.

This drunken mess was too dizzy.

Curtis lifted the brick high above his head.

Looked down upon Sullivan.

Licked his lips. Gave that same grin.

That fucking grin.

Just like Sullivan's father's.

And he brought the brick down.

Two gunshots fired.

The brick dropped to the side of Sullivan's head.

Another gunshot followed, then another after that.

Blood sprayed over Sullivan's face. It was in his mouth, in his eyes, in his nose. He had to snort it out, spit it out, blink it out.

It took Sullivan a moment to realise it wasn't his own blood.

Curtis flopped, his torso landing on Sullivan's head. Sullivan groaned and pushed the limp body away from him.

The sun hurt his eyes.

He looked to the side. At Curtis. A bullet hole in his head, and a few in his chest.

He looked up. Beside the van, Daniel stood, a gun in his hand.

A gun that was now aimed at Sullivan.

Sullivan watched Daniel as the world slowly lost its fuzziness, and he regained his sight. He had a pounding headache, and his body felt even heavier than it usually did, but he had enough about him to know that Daniel's gun was aimed at him.

Police cars swung around the end of the road. Sirens took over the street.

Sullivan just stared at Daniel, waiting to be arrested.

Then Daniel dropped the gun to his side, and distant shouts became clearer.

"That's Jay Sullivan!"

"Was he one of them?"

"Get him!"

Sullivan pushed himself to his knees. Police ran toward them, guns ready, eager to catch Sullivan.

He and Daniel focussed on each other. The agent's weary eyes and bruised face hung over a battered body. The man was strong, but even the strong suffer trauma. Sullivan knew a thing or two about it, and couldn't help but feel bad for what Daniel was going to face in the coming years.

Daniel stared back at Sullivan, recognising the man he thought he'd been hunting, and trying to separate him from the man who'd become his saviour.

Maybe Sullivan wasn't the man they thought he was.

Or maybe they'd just caught him on a good day.

Daniel nodded down the street. "Go," he said, his voice strong.

Sullivan used a nearby fire hydrant to pull himself to his feet.

"What?"

"I said go. I'll stall them."

Sullivan gazed at Daniel, bemused, and wondered why he'd done so much to save this agent. A day ago, Daniel would have been happy to see Sullivan put to death. But maybe that's how you change the world's perception of you — one person at a time.

"Hurry!" Daniel said.

The police were running toward them. He couldn't wait any longer. He turned and ran—at least, as much of a run as he could manage.

He turned left down a side street. Came across a manhole. Uncovered it. Looked over his shoulder.

They hadn't caught up yet.

He lowered himself inside and pulled the manhole cover over him.

It was pitch black. Thick water reached above his ankles. He felt furry things scurrying past his feet. The smell was rank.

He waited to see if anyone followed him down here.

No one did.

The thick sludge around his ankles felt disgusting, but he'd escaped through worse places.

He trudged onward, dragging his feet through dirty water, ignoring the creatures slithering past his shins.

Within twelve hours, he'd left the country.

# DAR ES SALAAM, TANZANIA

# CHAPTER FORTY-SIX

ONE WOULD HAVE THOUGHT A WHITE MAN IN TANZANIA would stick out. And he did. But sometimes it's better to stick out in a place where no one's hunting you, than blend into the background in a place where someone might know your face.

He walked along a single-track lane, much like the ones he'd find in the UK. Sometimes, when his father was in a truly foul mood, he'd run out of the house and find the nearest field and just walk for hours. People would pass him, look at him, and think how odd it was to see a child alone in the middle of nowhere. Then they'd carry on with their own lives.

A few sheep and goats ate grass. A few run-down buildings providing homes to families, in disrepair but much appreciated, lined the parts of his route that weren't lined with open fields.

After half an hour of walking, he left the fields and approached the water's edge, passing huts with sloping straw roofs and trees with many ferns, then past a grand building that looked quite out of place. Sullivan assumed it was a hotel built for people who consider themselves above locals. Sullivan's accumulated wealth from his time working for the government allowed him to stay in such places, but he did not object to the occasional hut or even a sleeping bag on the beach. He'd watch the darkness grow lighter until the sun rose. He'd listen to the locals getting drunk and the tourists discussing how differently people lived in such countries.

No matter where he was, he'd been somewhere more dangerous. He could handle himself, but he never needed to. Such countries were never as dangerous as richer countries made them out to be.

He left the tourist destinations full of locals trying to sell things to strangers. He walked past the rocky slopes that led toward the water, which was a shade of blue you'd never find in the UK. He walked along a small pier toward the ocean, passing couples on benches and children peering over the edge, their faces in awe. They were only a metre or so higher than the water's surface, but a child could make an adventure out of anything.

He reached the end of the pier and sat on the nearest bench. Most people didn't walk out this far. A nearby shack sold beers and snacks, and he asked for a lager. He found great peace in a place like this, but he still needed beer; an alcoholic doesn't change that easily.

Once he'd settled, and drunk the first beautiful sip of a cold beer on a hot day, he took out the laptop and opened it. He'd saved a few videos from an English news website when he'd passed through Eastern Europe a few days ago, but was worried he'd been sighted and had to keep moving. It wasn't until he'd passed through Kazakhstan that he realised no one was interested.

He placed the headphones in his ears, took another sip of beer, and pressed play as a woman reported on the news, the caption telling him she was the Washington correspondent. The White House sat proudly behind her.

"It has been a week since what the president referred to as a domestic terrorist attack, and the devastation is still being felt across the country," she spoke in perfect queen's English. "People continue to lay wreaths at the English embassy in New York to pay tribute to the twenty-six people who lost their lives, and on the streets leading up to the White House, where a member of the white supremacy group that called themselves White Avengers attempted to set an African American FBI agent on fire. The FBI agent himself, Daniel Winstead, spoke to the press for the first time this morning."

The picture changed to that of Daniel. His arm was in a sling, his eye was swollen, and he sat in an armchair beside a crutch. The injuries were clear—but the worst pain would be simmering beneath the surface, waiting to come out when Daniel least expected it.

"The experience has been... troubling, to say the least... What I witnessed in that embassy will stay with me forever. I can still smell the kerosene on my skin, and I still expect to be in that van every time I wake up."

Sullivan bowed his head. The nightmares were the worst. He was used to the disorientation of waking up, expecting to be in a cellar or a pit or a torture chamber, only to find that he was on the same mattress he fell asleep on.

The experience in the embassy had played on Sullivan's mind. He'd ruminated over whether he could have done more, and often imagined him changing his actions in a way that may have prevented so many people from dying. Then he'd try to think about other things. He'd add the guilt to the mountains of guilt he already held; it could have its turn some other day.

After all, this wasn't the first time he'd come face to face with mortality.

"And what would you say to the men who did this?" the reporter asked.

Daniel seemed to consider this deeply, before responding, "Nothing. They are dead."

"But there are many who harbour the same beliefs. In fact, whilst many other white supremacy groups have referred to these terrorists as monsters, many have called them heroes. What would you have to say to them?"

"What would I have to say to them..."

Daniel looked down. He took his time. He frowned, then smiled, then frowned again. Eventually, he looked up, and stared directly down the camera lens.

"I would say nothing," he answered. "I would listen."

"You would listen? But they hate you. Why would you listen to them?"

"Because no one does. These kids search for an identity, and they find it in the wrong place. They join something bigger than them, and they attack another group, and then that group attacks back, and we all think we're on the right side, until eventually so many people are dead that we've forgotten who the sides are anymore. So yes, they might hate me. But my point of view would do nothing to change that. So I would ask them one simple question: what was it that made you this angry? And then I would say nothing else until they'd finished talking."

Sullivan smiled. It was a good answer.

"And what of the rumours that Jay Sullivan, the notorious assassin who betrayed his own government, was involved with the White Avengers? What would you have to say to that?"

Daniel looked confused. "Jay who?"

"Jay Sullivan."

Daniel shrugged. "Was he there?"

"CCTV caught him being—"

"No one knows why Jay Sullivan has done the things he's done. I think we can say that for certain. Just as I can say for certain that, whilst this man may be many things, he is, without a doubt, not a racist."

"As in, he kills indiscriminately?"

"As in, he is an enigma, and we will never know what goes on inside his head – but I am sure it has nothing to do with the White Avengers."

The picture cut back to the original news reporter.

"The president declared a day of mourning on—"

Sullivan stopped the video. Closed the laptop lid. Wondered what it would be like to dive into such a clear, blue ocean. One day, he would love to go to the bottom and see just how deep it was. For now, however, he was done with diving into water.

Once he'd finished his beer, he returned the glass and nodded his thanks to the man in the shack. He walked back along the wooden pier and continued along the shore. His feet carried him along the rocky edge until he came to a small beach, where he sat and enjoyed the sound of the waves.

This was difficult to do.

Whenever he sat still, his memories would haunt him. Any opportunity to rest would be an opportunity for his mind to replay the worst moments of his life, which was also the end of many other people's.

A woman screaming for her husband's survival. A man's blood spraying over a suit sleeve. The smell of smoke as he left a building ablaze.

He didn't fight the thoughts. He'd caused so much pain that he didn't deserve to sit here in peace and tranquillity and enjoy it. Often, he considered ending his life, but two things forced him to prolong the suffering—the thought that he didn't deserve for the trauma to end, and the prospect of one day reuniting with his estranged daughter. Should she ever need his help, he would hate not to be there for her.

And so he sat there until the sun set, trying to gain pleasure in his perpetual solitude, and trying to ignore the memories that kept reminding him who he was.

He stayed there for hours, and in that time, he had a single moment—just one—where he found peace. A break from the thoughts. An absence of the evil he had committed.

A moment where he felt good for something he'd done, even if he had to do awful things to achieve it.

Then the moment passed, and the pain resumed, and he stood, unable to sit still any longer. If he kept walking, maybe he could convince his tired mind to let go of what he once was and concentrate on what he could be.

But the future wasn't for the Jay Sullivans of the world; it was for the Daniel Winsteads.

And, thankfully, Daniel Winstead was still alive to help those who need it.

At least that was one thing Jay Sullivan had given this world—a man who could truly do something remarkable. A man who could be known for the right choices.

That would be enough to allow Sullivan to sleep peacefully, if only for one night.

# WOULD YOU LIKE A FREE BOOK?

Join Ed Grace's mailing list and get FREE and EXCLUSIVE novella that tells the story of how Jay Sullivan was recruited to be an assassin...

Join at www.edgraceauthor.com/sign-up

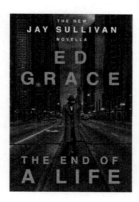

# ED
# GRACE

## ASSASSIN DOWN

A
Jay
Sullivan
Thriller

# ED
# GRACE

## KILL THEM QUICKLY

A
Jay
Sullivan
Thriller

# ED GRACE

## THE BARS THAT HOLD ME

A
Jay
Sullivan
Thriller

# ED
# GRACE

## A DEADLY WEAPON

A
Jay
Sullivan
Thriller

Printed in Great Britain
by Amazon